"You seem to know the McIvers well."

Chad's eyes raked Andrea's face. "Doesn't it disturb you that this Andy character beats little Hugo?"

"What?" Andrea gasped. "Did Hugo tell you that?"

"He did. His house backs onto my property, you know—that's how I met him. I caught him fishing in my pond. The poor kid was starving, and it was obvious he hadn't had a decent meal in weeks."

"That's not true," Andrea protested. What she wouldn't say to her brother when she got home!

Chad swerved the Land Rover to avoid a deep pothole. "Well, it is according to Hugo. I tell you, Miss—whatever your name is—when I get my hands on this Andy of his, I'll make the man wish he'd never been born!"

Books by Rosemary Badger

HARLEQUIN ROMANCES
2617—CORPORATE LADY
2629—A GIRL CALLED ANDY

These books may be available at your local bookseller.

For a free catalog listing all titles currently available,
send your name and address to:

Harlequin Reader Service
P.O. Box 52040, Phoenix, AZ 85072-2040
Canadian address: P.O. Box 2800, Postal Station A,
5170 Yonge St., Willowdale, Ont. M2N 5T5

A Girl Called Andy

Rosemary Badger

Harlequin Books

TORONTO • NEW YORK • LONDON
AMSTERDAM • PARIS • SYDNEY • HAMBURG
STOCKHOLM • ATHENS • TOKYO • MILAN

Original hardcover edition published in 1984
by Mills & Boon Limited

ISBN 0-373-02629-3

Harlequin Romance first edition July 1984

CHAPTER ONE

'Hi, sweetie. Where's Hugo?' asked Andrea of nine-year-old Melissa, who was busy doing her homework at the kitchen table.

Melissa jumped up from the table and ran to hug her sister. 'Andy, you're home!' she squealed. 'But you're so late, I was beginning to get worried.'

'Sorry, pet, but I had a bit of trouble with the car. Darn thing wouldn't start after I got some groceries,' Andrea explained, placing the bag of groceries on the table and shrugging out of her coat. 'Where's Hugo?' she asked again. 'Why isn't he doing his homework?'

'He's gone fishing,' Melissa told her uninterestedly, as she rummaged through the bag of groceries searching for treats.

'Fishing!' Andrea exploded. 'In this freezing weather and at this hour? Why, that little monkey! I told him to come straight home after school and do his homework. He has a cold, he had me up practically the whole night last night with his coughing. Where has he gone fishing?' she asked, running a hand through her thick chestnut-coloured hair.

'I think he went over to the Manor. He said something about hanging around until he met the new owner,' Melissa shrugged, as she hungrily eyed some chocolate chip biscuits before placing them aside and taking out a packet of sausages. 'Not sausages again!' she wailed in disgust. 'We've had sausages for tea practically every night this week!'

Andrea took the sausages from her. 'Stop exaggerating,' she said. 'We've only had them once this week. Besides, you used to love them.'

'Not any more, I don't. I hope Hugo catches some fish for our tea. I love fish.'

'You used to hate fish,' Andrea reminded her with a smile, her soft hazel eyes bright with amusement. 'And Hugo is going to catch a lot more than fish when he gets home. I told him yesterday he wasn't to go over to the Manor.' She glanced at the empty wood box by the slow-combustion stove. 'Look at that!' she sighed. 'As usual he's forgotten to fill it. Would you get a few pieces of wood, Melissa, while I change out of my clothes, then I'll get the fire started before I go and look for him.'

'All right, Andy, but I don't see why I should have to do Hugo's chores,' Melissa grumbled, as she started towards the door. Andrea watched her go and then went upstairs to get into a pair of old jeans. Ever since their parents and two brothers had died in a car crash, she had assumed full responsibility for her younger brother and sister. The family home had been heavily mortgaged and Andrea was forced to sell it. With the money left over she managed to finish her degree at teacher training college and pay for part-time help to care for the children. Then, with her degree in her hand, she and the children had moved from Sydney to make a fresh start in Tasmania.

That was a year ago, when Andrea was barely

twenty. A part-time teaching job at a remedial school in Hobart provided her with the money she and the children needed to live, and after careful research and with plenty of luck the little trio had found a small home in the Huon Valley. The place was pretty run down, but the rent was cheap and the children were able to have a few pets and a vegetable garden which kept down the food bill.

But lately Hugo had become a handful, hardly ever doing what he was told, and often, like his going over to the Manor, was becoming more and more disobedient.

After Andrea had made the fire in the slow-combustion stove she left Melissa setting the table while she set out to look for Hugo. Melissa had said he had gone to the Manor, so she headed in the direction of the Manor pond. A fringe of apple trees separated their house from the boundaries of the Manor estate, and as Andrea trudged through the tall grasses which grew between the trees she eventually came to a small clearing where she had a good view of the pond.

Hugo was crouched by the side of the pond looking very small and forlorn. She was about to call out to him when a movement caught her attention. A man was making his way towards him, in long, forceful strides. She saw Hugo look up to see the man and then calmly turn back to his fishing, as if he had every right to be there. Andrea wondered if she should rush out from where she was hidden by the trees and try to defend Hugo's actions or if she should allow Hugo to face up to the man himself.

She knew that the man must be the new owner of

the Manor. From where she stood she could see he was extremely tall and there was something lordly about the way he carried himself. She was too far away to distinguish his features, but she could see he had black hair and very dark eyes. He was well built, his shoulders seeming to go on for ever under the tweed fabric of his jacket. As the man approached Hugo, Andrea felt her heartbeat quicken, for there was an arrogance, a sort of ruthlessness about the man that frightened her.

But she needn't have worried. He was treating Hugo with a dignified courtesy which was far more than she felt her brother deserved in the circumstances. The man said something to Hugo and then squatted beside him, Hugo moving just a bit to give him room. Obviously they were discussing fishing techniques, a subject which was one of Hugo's favourites. Hugo handed the man the rod and Andrea watched while he made a few practice castings before he bent his head closer to Hugo's, explaining something about the line.

Hugo was nodding his head and Andrea could hear the sudden burst of laughter pour from her little brother's throat at something the man was telling him. She became comfortable watching them. The man certainly seemed to have a way with children, and she found she couldn't take her eyes from him. She still couldn't see what he looked like, but she could see enough to make her realise his incredibly dark features must make for a very handsome specimen!

He was gentle too. She could tell that by the way he was treating Hugo, and once he put his arm around the boy's shoulders, the way a father would to a small son he thought was cold. And it was cold. Andrea was shivering in her thin winter jacket and she knew it must be even colder sitting by the pond.

The line was cast out once more and then she heard Hugo shouting with excitement. The line was reeled in and Andrea saw a plump fish dangling on the end. Obviously the advice Hugo had received had been good, she thought. Her yellow laundry bucket was beside Hugo and she watched while he extracted the fish from his line and casually tossed it into the bucket, before getting to his feet. Now that he was standing, Andrea could see he was only wearing a short-sleeved T-shirt. After all her warnings about dressing warmly, he had forgotten to put on his jacket. Anxiety mingled with anger. How long had he sat there in the freezing cold, with nothing but a T-shirt to keep him warm? She would be up half the night looking after him, and he probably wouldn't be well enough for school in the morning.

The man was still speaking to Hugo, and Andrea smiled when she saw them shaking hands. Hugo would like that, she knew. The boy turned and pointed in the direction of their house and she saw the man nod, before picking up the bucket and handing it to him. Hugo kept turning back to wave as he made his way across the meadow, the bright yellow pail bobbing by his side.

Andrea took a last glance at the man, before turning towards the house. She didn't want Hugo to know she had been spying on him, but she was curious to know what the man had said and she was confident her brother would relate their conversation in detail once he got home. But her parting look at the man troubled her somewhat. The thrust of his shoulders, and the way his hands were stuffed in his trouser pockets, indicated anger, but somehow she didn't believe he was upset because Hugo had fished from his pond, but rather that his anger was directed at something or somebody else.

'He's coming,' she announced to Melissa, when she got back home.

'Was he fishing like I said?' Melissa enquired, putting bread on the table.

'Yes—and without his jacket on, too!'

'I hope he caught some. I sure would rather have fish than sausages.'

'Hi, everybody!' shouted Hugo, opening the kitchen door with a grand flourish and holding the yellow bucket high overhead. 'Bet you can't guess what I've got in this here bucket?'

'Bet you didn't catch any fish?' Melissa teased, reaching for the bucket. 'Bet the new owner of the Manor ran you off his property, and it would serve you right if he did!'

Hugo ignored her, going straight to Andrea. 'Look what I brought you, Andy,' he said, pride ringing through his voice as he held the pail for her to see. 'I brought you some fish!'

She looked down into his face and her heart swelled with love. She knew how much he still missed his father, but lately he had begun acting peculiarly, helping out in ways which usually proved disastrous—like taking fish from someone else's pond, rather than keeping the wood box filled. He was looking up at her, his big blue eyes begging her to be proud of him, while all she saw was that he was cold and that his thin little shoulders were shivering under the cotton T-shirt. 'You're cold,' she said, placing a hand on his head and tossling the blond curls. 'I warned you to put your jacket on before you went out to play. In fact, I told you to stay indoors. You have a cold . . .'

'Play?' He shrugged away from her in disgust. 'I wasn't *playing*—I was *fishing*! Look what I got you,' he commanded once more, holding up the pail.

Andrea peered into the pail, expecting to see the single fish she had watched Hugo catch. Instead, there were several. 'Good heavens! Don't tell me you took all these from the Manor pond?' she asked worriedly.

'I did,' he declared proudly. 'Eleven of them!'

'But, Hugo,' she said, grabbing his arm and leading him to a chair, 'you told me the other day that you'd seen the Manor pond being stocked with trout.'

'I did. The men from the fisheries did it.'

'Then these are *all* trout?'

'Sure they are.'

'Hugo! Do you realise how much it must have cost to have that pond filled with trout? Plenty, I can assure you, and they weren't put there for the benefit of neighbours. When Melissa told me she thought you might have gone fishing, I didn't think for a minute that you would actually have the nerve to take fish from other people's ponds. Now you and Melissa put them back, and I don't want to ever hear you were over at that Manor again. We had enough trouble with the previous owner over those apples you took. Let's not start anything with the new owner.'

Andrea turned and put the pan on the stove in readiness for the sausages, then went to the fridge to take out the eggs. 'Well, you heard me,' she said to the children. 'Get your jackets on and put those trout back!'

Hugo and Melissa exchanged glances, and Melissa put her hand to her mouth to stifle her giggles.

'We can't put them back,' Hugo drawled. 'They're dead!'

Andrea stared at him and then at the trout. She had wanted to teach Hugo a lesson, but obviously this wasn't to be the time! 'I didn't actually mean in the pond,' she mumbled. 'I meant to the Manor, of course.'

'I met the man who's bought the Manor,' Hugo announced. 'He even shook my hand, and that was after I fished his pond. He seemed real pleased I'd fished his pond and said I could fish it once a month if I only caught eleven.'

'Why would anyone want to shake your hand, Hugo McIver? I bet you're lying,' accused Melissa.

'I'm not lying,' Hugo insisted. 'He introduced himself to me and asked who I was and where I lived.'

'What's his name, then?' Melissa asked.

'Chad Hallister,' Hugo announced proudly. 'He said he writes books.'

'Chad Hallister!' Andrea repeated the name. 'I've heard around town that it was an author who'd bought the old Manor, but I didn't think it would be someone quite so famous.'

'You mean Chad Hallister is famous?' Hugo beamed. He turned to Melissa. 'Just think,' he teased, 'I've shaken hands with someone famous!' He turned back to Andrea. 'Do you think I've read any of his books, Andy?'

'I doubt it,' she chuckled. 'None of his stories appear in comics. But you will read them when you're older, I should imagine. He writes wild adventure stories, usually with exotic settings and backgrounds.' She looked at the trout still in the bucket. 'No wonder he can afford to stock his pond with trout!'

'Gee, Hugo,' sighed Melissa, 'I wish I'd gone with you. Tell us what he looks like.'

Hugo was fairly swaggering with self-importance as he pondered Melissa's request. 'Like a man!' he finally answered, and Andrea suppressed a smile while Melissa urged him to continue.

'What colour hair?' she demanded to know.

'Black.'

'What colour eyes?'

'Black.'

'Hah!' jeered Melissa. 'I bet you're going to say he has a black beard as well.'

'No,' sighed Hugo, 'no beard. Too bad, eh? I like beards.'

'Well, it looks like you've been granted your wish, Melissa,' Andrea broke in. 'We'll leave the sausages for another night and eat trout tonight.' She picked up the fish, dreading the thought of cleaning them. 'I wonder why Mr Hallister suggested eleven fish,' she mused aloud, 'and why at the end of the month.' She eyed Hugo suspiciously. 'Are you sure that's what he said?'

'Yup! He counted the fish I had in the bucket and asked me if eleven was enough for my family. I said it was, even with Bingo having one. He asked me who Bingo was and I told him he was my dog. He said to make sure Bingo got his fill. Wasn't that nice of him?'

Andrea grinned. 'Super,' she agreed. 'But we'll have to pay Mr Hallister for these fish. We don't want the Lord of the Manor to think we're in need of his charity . . . for ourselves or our dog!'

'Do you think he really is a lord?' gushed Melissa, who was at the romantic stage of her young life.

'He probably thinks he is,' muttered Andrea as she began cleaning the trout. 'Living in that great big Manor and probably with servants catering to his every whim and fancy.'

'I'm going to live in a Manor when I grow up,' prophesied Hugo, as he began helping his sister with the fish.

'If you don't end up in prison first!' laughed Andrea, giving him a playful nudge. 'But I meant what I said before,' she added on a more serious note. 'I don't want you hanging around the Manor. Mr Hallister must be a very busy man and he certainly won't appreciate being disturbed by you.' She turned to Melissa. 'That goes for you, too!'

Later that evening, with the dishes washed and put away, the ironing done and the school lunches made and in the fridge for the children to take to school the next day, Andrea sat at the kitchen table working on her finances.

'What are you doing, Andy?' a sleepy voice asked her, and she looked up to see Hugo standing in the doorway.

'What's the matter?' she asked. 'Can't you sleep?'

'My throat hurts,' he complained, 'and every time I cough, I wake up.'

'What did you expect?' she asked wearily, 'sitting without your jacket on in this cold weather, and all for the sake of a few fish!'

'It wasn't just for the fish, Andy. I wanted to meet Mr Hallister.'

Chad Hallister, she thought, pushing away her papers. Hugo had talked of nothing else the whole evening, until even Melissa had grown tired of listening about Hugo's great, if not sudden, friendship with the man.

'Well, I can't give you any more medication,' she told him. 'You've already had the prescribed amounts.' She looked at his flushed face. 'How about if I put the vapouriser on for you? That might help.'

'No, it won't,' he answered. 'It never does. I think I had better stay home from school tomorrow,' he suggested hopefully.

'And I think you'd better go to school tomorrow,' she countered smilingly. 'You'll be a lot better off at school than fishing in Mr Hallister's pond. Now get yourself off to bed or your teacher will be sending another note home, saying you slept through your English class again.'

He looked at the papers on the table. 'What's that for?' he asked. 'Why have you written down all those figures?'

'For the car,' she answered. 'It wouldn't start after I got some groceries. I had to have it towed to the garage, and I was just trying to calculate how much it's going to cost for repairs.'

'Plenty, I'll bet. My friend's dad had to have his car fixed, and he said it cost in the hundreds!'

Exactly what she was afraid of. Trust Hugo to put it so bluntly! 'Well, your friend's dad probably has a much bigger car than us,' she told him, getting up from the table. 'I'll find out tomorrow exactly what it will cost, but it shouldn't be much.' She gave him a hug. 'I'll have to take the early bus into work,' she said, 'so I'll be gone by the time you and Melissa wake up. Make sure you remember your lunches in the fridge—and don't forget to wear your jacket.'

'I wish you didn't have to work,' Hugo said miserably, looking up at her. 'Can't you stay home tomorrow?'

She hugged him closer. 'I wish I could, sweetie, but you know I can't.'

'When I get bigger,' he declared fiercely, 'I'll work and you won't have to. I'll buy you a big house just like the Manor House and I'll buy you a new car so you won't always be worrying about it breaking down and having to take buses everywhere.'

He was crying, and she waited awhile before saying softly, 'I know you will, sweetie, but for now let's just be grateful we have each other. You and Melissa are lucky to have each other during the day when I'm not home and I'm lucky to have you and

Melissa to come home to in the evenings.'

With Hugo in bed once more, Andrea tidied up and then went to bed. Several times she awakened to the children coughing, getting up to fetch them glasses of water and to give them their medicine. When morning finally arrived, she felt as though she had hardly been asleep. She dressed, had a quick breakfast, made some porridge for the children and left for work. The garage was open, but the mechanic told her he hadn't had a chance to look over her car. Minutes later, Andrea was standing at the bus stop in front of the post office waiting for her bus to arrive and hoping nothing serious was wrong with the car and that this would be the only day she would have to worry about buses.

The day dragged by. She was worried about the children, wondering if perhaps she should have stayed home to look after them, instead of forcing them to go to school. But the headmaster frowned upon his teachers . . . especially the part-time teachers . . . taking days off. With two children to support, she didn't dare stray from his favour and risk losing her job.

Ordinarily, she finished work at four, but there was a teachers' meeting and she wasn't out until five, which meant the bus to the Valley only went as far as Huonville, before turning on its way to Cygnet. She would have to either walk to Franklin where their little house was, a distance of at least five miles, or hope to get a lift with someone she knew. Either way, it meant she would be home much later than usual, and with the children sick, the thought filled her with despair.

When the bus let her off at Huonville, she walked towards the shop where she had jackets on lay-by for Hugo and Melissa. The sudden cold change in weather had caught everyone by surprise and she still had a few more instalments to make before she could have them. She wished she could pay them off and take them home tonight, but a quick check in her wallet told her she couldn't. It was pay-day tomorrow, but as usual her salary was carefully budgeted, and even allowing for more corners cut, it would be impossible to have the jackets paid off for at least a few more weeks. Going into the shop, she made another payment, checked how much she still owed and then left, burrowing her head into her suit jacket against the fierce cold. Not watching where she was going, she ploughed into someone directly in front of her and was sent sprawling on to the footpath. Almost immediately, strong hands gripped her arms and she was helped to her feet.

Dazed, she stared into a pair of incredibly black eyes—eyes so fiercely black that she felt trapped by the sheer potency of their glare. Andrea felt a shiver race up and then down her spine. Her lips parted as though to speak, but she found she couldn't utter a word. The man's hands were still on her arms and through the thin fabric of her jacket she could feel his hands burning her flesh! Black brows were drawn into a frown as the man continued to stare at her, his eyes finally moving from hers to travel across her face, examining her features in detail as though committing them to memory.

He was very tall, her brain in its confusion man-

aged to inform her. Broad shoulders blocked out
the street, making her feel she was quite alone with
this stranger. His hands moved slowly down her
arms, leaving a trail of gooseflesh behind them, and
when she shivered once more, he smiled, teeth
startling white against the darkness of his skin.

'What's your name?' he asked her, with a bold-
ness that shocked her to her senses, allowing her to
shrug away from his hands and freeing her from the
power his touch held for her. 'What's your name?'
he asked again, his eyes slightly mocking as she
stepped away from him, her eyes never leaving his
face.

'None of your business!' she finally managed to
gasp, wondering as she did why she had even
bothered to answer.

Her reply didn't deter him. In fact, she had the
weird sensation he had expected an answer like that
from her. Who was he? she wondered frantically,
as he stepped closer to her, once more grabbing her
arm. His fingers closed around her wrist and rested
against her racing pulse. He looked down at his
hand holding her wrist and smiled.

Andrea yanked her wrist away, rubbing it as
though it had been burnt. 'Let me pass,' she hissed.
'You have no right blocking the footpath!'

'You're right,' he amazed her by agreeing. 'And
judging from the speed you were walking, you must
be in a great hurry to get to wherever you are
going.'

'Well, yes,' she admitted, wondering at his
change of attitude. 'I'm late getting home.'

'Could I drive you? Or do you have a car?'

'I'm walking, thanks,' she answered primly, starting to move past him.

But she wasn't to escape so easily. 'You're certain you're all right?' he enquired. 'You landed pretty heavily on that footpath.'

He made her sound like a clumsy elephant. 'Quite all right, thank you,' she answered stiffly, and this time when she moved away, he let her.

Andrea could feel his eyes behind her as she hurried down the street. She had only been walking for about ten minutes when a Land Rover cruised up beside her. There weren't any lights, apart from a few houses, and her heart skipped with fear at the vehicle she didn't recognise. The driver leaned over and opened the door. 'Hop in!' a deep voice growled the command.

Helplessly, Andrea stared into the face of the stranger she had just been talking to. 'N-no,' she whispered, stumbling backwards. Just then the rain, which had been falling on and off the whole of the day, started again.

'Get in, or I'll drag you in.' The voice was entirely without patience, and Andrea guessed she had better do as she was told, or suffer the humiliation of being dragged, as he had warned, into the vehicle.

The Land Rover was warm after the cold, but still she shivered. He reached for the appropriate button and more warm air circled freely about her. She stole a glance at his face, wondering still who he might be and if she would ever arrive home safely. Every horrid story she had heard about the fate of women hitch-hikers circulated in her brain.

'You must live in Franklin.' It was a statement not a question.

'Yes,' she answered.

His eyes gleamed down at her. 'Not very talkative, are you?' When she didn't answer, he chuckled. 'Not very sensible, either. What was the idea walking alone on this road? I offered you a lift before. Why didn't you accept?'

Andrea stirred uncomfortably in her seat. 'I accepted,' she mumbled.

'Only under threat! Why didn't you accept in town and spare your feet the hardship of walking in those ridiculous shoes you women insist on wearing?'

My God, she thought, don't tell me he even noticed the shoes on my feet! She looked across at him and he met her glance. Those eyes of his wouldn't miss a thing, she decided.

'I like walking,' she insisted.

His disbelieving laugh swept over her, and under shelter of the darkened interior, she smiled.

'Even on a night such as this?' he scoffed. 'Why, it's freezing out there, and it wouldn't surprise me if that rain turned to snow before very long.'

'*Especially* on a night such as this,' she persisted in saying.

The vehicle rode over a crater in the road and the jostling it caused permitted a parcel she hadn't noticed beside her slip to the floor. Andrea bent to retrieve it, placing it back on the seat.

'That's something for a great little friend of mine,' the stranger told her. 'Do you know anything about kids?'

'A . . . little,' she admitted.

She felt his eyes on her face, but avoided his glance. 'You're too young to know much about them, but if you wouldn't mind, I'd like your opinion on that jacket. Unwrap it and tell me if it would fit a ten-year-old. The saleslady assured me it would, but he's such a scrawny little fellow, I have my doubts. It might be too big.'

Andrea undid the wrapping. Inside was a jacket. She had seen it many times in the same store where she had jackets for Hugo and Melissa on lay-by. But this jacket was a much better one, and much, much more expensive. Her hands sank into the fleece of the lining. She knew it had a hood and big pockets and that it was trimmed with bright red piping.

'It's a beautiful jacket,' she said at last, tucking it back into its wrapping. 'Your little friend should like it very much.'

'Sure hope so. His name is Hugo—Hugo McIver. You might know him, he lives in Franklin. Poor little guy is terrified of his guardian.' The stranger turned to stare into Andrea's horrified face. 'His guardian's name is Andy . . . Andy McIver!'

CHAPTER TWO

ANDREA'S horrified eyes studied the man's face.
Chad Hallister! Heavens, she thought, why hadn't
she realised it before? Hugo's description of Chad
Hallister rebounded in her brain. He looks like a
man, Hugo had said, and indeed the child had been
right. A man like no other she had ever met! A man
so potently male that just sitting beside him was
sufficient to send her pulses racing.

Black hair, Hugo had said, and again he had
been right. Hair so black it could have been pluck-
ed from a raven's wing. She was still staring at him
when he diverted his attention from the road, to
give her a sideways glance. Eyes so fiercely black
they could have been pieces of coal.

Her eyes wavered under the intensity of his look.
She looked down at her hands folded on her lap.
She had seen him yesterday while he stood talking
to Hugo at the pond. But the distance between
them had been too great for her to examine him in
detail. He had been dressed in some sort of tweed
jacket with matching trousers, totally opposite to
what he was wearing now—a bulky suede jacket
and faded, well used blue jeans. She hadn't seen his
face, but she remembered now that it was his
attitude that had interested her. He had seemed
angry. What on earth had Hugo said to him . . . and
about her, of all people!

'Do you know the McIvers?' he asked her now.

Andrea gave a little cough, clearing her throat. 'Well, yes,' she answered reluctantly, 'actually, I do.'

'What's this Andy character like? A drunkard, I'll bet.'

'Well, no. I've never heard *that* said about . . . about Andy McIver.'

Chad shrugged his broad shoulders. 'It's amazing no one has done something about that family.'

'What do you mean?' she asked weakly.

'Hugo, for instance. It's obvious he isn't being properly cared for.'

'Why, Hugo receives *excellent* care!'

Chad turned towards her, surprised by her vehement denial of his suggestion. 'How do you know?' he asked.

'I . . . I just know, that's all,' she managed to mumble, then added. 'Well, it might not be excellent, but it's pretty damned good.'

His eyes raked her face. 'You seem to know the family well. Doesn't it disturb you that Andy beats little Hugo?'

Her eyes widened in horror. 'No!' she gasped. 'Did Hugo tell you that?'

'He did. I've just bought the old Manor in Franklin . . . by the way,' he grinned, his teeth a flash of white in the darkness of the vehicle, 'my name is Hallister . . . Chad Hallister.'

This could have been the time for Andrea to reveal her identity, but when she made no attempt to do so, Chad's grin merely widened and a wicked gleam appeared in his eyes. 'Still not ready to tell

me your name eh? Well, it doesn't matter, I'll find
out sooner or later.' He turned his attention back to
the road.

'Hugo's house backs on to the Manor,' he continued to inform her. 'That's how I happened to
meet him. I caught him fishing in my trout pond.
The poor little kid was starving, and by the look of
him, it was easy to see he hadn't had a decent meal
in weeks.'

'But that's not true,' Andrea again protested. 'I
happen to know that Hugo eats very good meals.'

'How do you know that? Are you there when he
eats?' he asked sarcastically.

'Yes! Often!'

'Then obviously you've never been there just
before pay-day.'

'Pay-day?'

Chad Hallister swerved to avoid a deep pothole.
'According to Hugo, Andy only gets paid once a
month. Apparently the money runs out, probably
through careless spending on Andy's part and
there's nothing left to buy food. I've given Hugo
permission to fish once a month, so at least I'll
know he won't go hungry.'

So that was why Hugo said he could fish once a
month, she thought. The little traitor! She would
have a few words to say to him when she got home!

'That's very generous of you,' she murmured,
glad he couldn't see her cheeks burning with
embarrassment. What *was* Hugo up to? she wondered, squirming in her seat.

Chad Hallister pushed the compliment aside, not
even bothering to respond to it. Andrea stole a

glance at his profile and was startled by the grim set
of his features. There were hard, angry lines about
his mouth and there was sufficient light from the
dashboard to reveal narrowed eyes. He was
obviously, genuinely, extremely concerned about
Hugo and what he believed was the poor boy's
plight.

Up till now, Andrea hadn't taken any of it
seriously, simply because she knew none of it was
true. She had even been slightly amused by Chad
Hallister's concern for Hugo and had thought how
funny it would be to see the expression on his face
when she finally told him that she was Andy.

But now a faint uneasiness stirred within her.
Chad Hallister was rich and famous, maybe even
powerful. Could he cause trouble for her and the
children? Perhaps she *wasn't* caring for them well
enough. Hugo was on the thin side, but in contrast
Melissa was fairly plump. They both ate the same
amount. Hugo was just naturally thin, and besides,
he was so active, he ran all his fat off.

Even the idea of her beating Hugo was ludicrous.
She had never even slapped him, never mind
beaten him! But obviously Hugo had allowed Mr
Hallister to believe she had. She couldn't believe
Hugo to be so disloyal.

'Did . . . did Hugo actually tell you that . . . that
Andy beats him?'

She saw his hands tighten around the steering
wheel, his knuckles white.

'Twice, as a matter of fact. Yesterday when I was
talking to him he said he'd better race home or
Andy would give him a thrashing if he was late.

Then today he came over after school. He said Andy would kill him for coming over to the Manor, that he'd been warned to stay away.' He peered at her sideways. 'Obviously this Andy character doesn't want me to find out too much about them.'

Arrogant swine! she thought, wisely keeping her opinion about the man to herself.

'Perhaps Andy doesn't want Hugo to bother you,' she suggested instead. That Hugo! she fumed. She had warned him repeatedly to stay away from the Manor. 'After all, you've just moved in. There must be lots for you to do, without having a little boy underfoot.'

But Chad Hallister wasn't to be persuaded. 'No, it goes deeper than that. You know how cold this weather has been. Well, yesterday he was fishing with only a short-sleeved shirt on. He was shivering, his lips were blue, and to top it off, he has a cold. The kid should have been in a nice warm bed, instead of outside poaching fish for the family meal.'

She bit back an angry retort, smiled sweetly, then came out with what she hoped would put an end to the matter. 'The McIvers aren't the sort of people who *poach*. If I know Andy McIver, which I do,' she assured him, 'you'll get paid for those fish. Oh, perhaps not in cold, hard cash, the McIvers have never pretended to have much of that, but you will get paid. They grow their own vegetables. You'll probably wake up one morning to find a few turnips on your doorstep.'

He chuckled. 'Turnips? I detest the things!'

'Well, maybe it will be something else. It could be a carrot . . . maybe even two carrots.'

He laughed aloud. 'You seem to like this Andy McIver.'

'Oh, I do, I do!'

'Even knowing he beats his kids?'

She shook her head. 'I don't believe for an instant that Andy would ever lay a finger on either Hugo or Melissa.'

'Melissa? Is that the little girl's name? I've seen her playing, but I have as yet to meet her.'

That's because Melissa is obedient and stays away from the Manor like she's been told, Andrea felt like saying.

'Perhaps you will. Hugo will probably drag her over to meet you some day,' she said.

His laugh was easy. 'So you think I've made too much out of my assumptions and from what Hugo has told me?'

'Yes, I do,' she answered quietly.

'But today he had on a pair of shorts. There were bruises on his legs. How would you explain that?'

'Sport. You know what little boys are like when they're playing. They can get pretty rough at times.'

She could tell by his silence that he still wasn't convinced, but she felt she was making some headway.

'Child abuse can take on many forms,' he answered slowly. 'I still say Hugo is being neglected. His clothing, for example. Imagine letting a kid out in this weather with shorts!'

She could imagine it. She had left before the

children were out of bed and obviously Hugo had
taken it into his head to wear shorts instead of his
long trousers, like he was supposed to do.

'Andy must not have known he was out in
shorts,' she defended herself. 'Anyway, you know
what children are like . . . they hardly ever feel the
cold.'

'He was cold . . . freezing!'

'Was . . . was he wearing his jacket?'

Chad Hallister glanced at her curiously. 'No.'

'But surely he has one,' she sighed, trying to
count how many times she had reminded Hugo
about wearing his jacket.

'He said he did, but that he didn't like wearing it
because it was too tight under the arms and that it
hurt.'

'And so you rushed right out and bought him
one,' she sighed. 'Didn't it occur to you that Andy
might have jackets on lay-by?'

'The kid needs a jacket now, not when it's no
longer cold. Anyway, Hugo didn't hold much store
by Andy being able to get him one. He had some
story about the car breaking down and in the garage
for repairs.' He shot her a cursory glance. 'Your
sympathies seem largely with Andy instead of with
Hugo who's in need of help. You've indicated
you're a frequent visitor at his home. I suggest you
go over there and listen to him cough. If he were my
kid, I'd get him to a doctor!'

'I'm surprised that you haven't already done so,'
she lashed back, worry and fear making her unreasonable. She glanced down at the jacket separ-
ating them. 'You have no right poking your nose

into other people's business. The McIvers don't
need and don't want your charity!'

Her outburst didn't perturb him in the least.
They had come into Franklin and he adjusted his
speed accordingly.

'Where to?' He asked casually, in a manner
which suggested he was truly a friend and not the
foe she thought him to be.

'The grocery shop, please.'

Chad Hallister pulled alongside the shop. 'I'll
wait for you,' he said.

'No!'

He gave her a strange look. 'No?' he enquired.

Andrea shifted uncomfortably in her seat. 'I
mean . . . no, thank you.'

He smiled. 'That's better,' he drawled, making
her feel like a rude ten-year-old.

'It's just that I could be a long time.'

He shrugged. 'I don't mind waiting.'

'No . . . no, please don't. It makes me . . .
nervous shopping while someone is waiting for me.'

His smile mocked her. 'Is that the only reason?'

Andrea reached up a slender hand to tuck a lock
of hair behind her ear. He watched the movement
with interest, noting the pink flush staining her
cheeks. 'Of course. What other reason could there
be?'

'None whatsoever,' he chuckled, reaching across
her to open the door.

There was nothing left for her to do except step
down from the Rover and disappear into the shop,
but strangely she felt unwilling to leave the company of this maddeningly arrogant man. Her eyes

swept up to meet his and she realised he had guessed her dilemma. Furious with herself for being so obvious, she quickly stepped down from the Rover, desperately searching her brain for something cutting to say. On the footpath she looked up at him, her hand on the door.

'What did you say your name was?' she enquired innocently. 'Chuck, wasn't it? Chuck something or other.' She squeezed her brows together in a show of concentration, then snapped her fingers. 'I've got it . . . Chuck Holster!'

'Chuck Holster sounds pretty good, but it's not my name.' His smile told her that he knew very well that she knew what his name was. 'Want to try again?' he quipped.

Damn him! she thought, hating his conceit and smug arrogance and his ability to outwit her at every turn. 'I just remembered,' she mumbled. 'It's Chad Hallister.'

'Good girl,' he drawled.

She gave a defiant toss of her head, wondering why she should even bother continuing with this ridiculous conversation.

'I've heard around the village that you're an author,' she said.

'Then you've heard correctly.'

'Must be an easy job,' she said offhandedly. 'Thinking up little ditties and scribbling them down on paper. Do you actually get paid for your little anecdotes?'

The grin spread slowly across his face. 'I do, and rather handsomely at that.'

Andrea hunched a shoulder and shook her head.

'It sure makes one wonder, doesn't it?' she asked sadly. 'That people will actually go out and pay good money to read your adventure stories.'

'How do you know I write adventure stories?' he asked, his eyes bright with amusement.

'Oh, I don't!' she answered quickly. 'I just happened to make a good guess.'

'Well, it so happens that my latest little "ditty" has taken six months of exhausting and dangerous research in the wilds of East Africa, not to mention the small fortune it cost to set up safaris, guides, equipment and transport. Add to that the months it will take to document my research, the several drafts to get it all in line, then the big write when it becomes a story.'

She was impressed, but it would be certain suicide to show it. 'Gosh!' she exclaimed. 'That sounds almost as hard as my job!'

He raised his brows expectantly. 'And what's your job?' he asked.

'I'm a schoolteacher,' it gave her great pleasure to inform him.

A black brow formed a majestic arch. 'Curious,' he drawled.

'Why?' she laughed. 'Because your jungle is in East Africa and mine is in the classroom? You know . . . the movie, *The Blackboard Jungle!*' she attempted to explain when he gave no indication of appreciating the comparison.

He was still staring at her with that same disbelieving look. 'No, I find it curious that you're a teacher, that's all.'

Andrea straightened her shoulders. 'Why should

you find that curious?' she demanded to know. 'I happen to be a very good teacher.'

'Oh, I wouldn't doubt that for an instant.'

'Well then, why is it curious?'

'Because Andy McIver happens to be a teacher as well!'

'Well, I would hardly call that *curious*,' she snapped, her cheeks suddenly pale. 'I would call it a coincidence.'

'Really?' he smiled, a slow mocking smile. 'How about if we call it a curious coincidence?'

Andrea backed away from the Rover. 'Oh, for heaven's sake, call it whatever you like. I've got shopping to do, surely you must have something to do as well. Why don't you go home and work on your book!'

With her shopping done and a quick visit to the garage about her car, Andrea finally made it home, prepared to do battle with Hugo. But the children were far too sick for anything other than some hot soup and a few soothing words. After getting them into bed, she lit the slow-combustion stove. The house was so cold she almost decided to make a fire in the lounge fireplace. But she was wary of the fireplace. It always smoked and never seemed to draw well. Sitting down at the kitchen table to do her school work, she thought of Chad Hallister and how he would handle the children.

She doubted he would give in to them the way she always seemed to do. Chad Hallister wasn't the kind of man who would jump to anyone's tune. Well, she owned reluctantly, maybe just a bit to Hugo.

Thinking about Chad, Andrea completely forgot about her school work, or of adding some more wood to the fire. When she finally realised the kitchen had grown cold, she snatched up some newspapers and with some kindling managed to get the fire going. She watched the fire blaze with new life for a while before shutting the door. She stood up and stretched. She was tired—hardly any sleep last night and probably not much more tonight.

Bingo was fast asleep by the stove and she didn't have the heart to wake him and put him outside. She decided he might as well remain where he was; at least one member of the family wouldn't be walking around tomorrow with bags under his eyes!

Upstairs, she made a last check on the children. Melissa stirred when Andrea put an extra blanket over her, and then started coughing. Andrea helped her to sit up and then held her while she sipped at some water. When the child was once more asleep, Andrea tiptoed into Hugo's room. His bedside lamp was on and under its glare she could see how flushed he was. Gently, she touched his cheek, alarmed at how much hotter he was now than he had been earlier. He moaned and rolled on to his side, his blue eyes opening for a second, then closing again.

Andrea decided she must get his fever down. Back downstairs she flew, racing up again with a pan of ice-cold water. For over an hour she bathed him, and during this time Hugo hardly seemed aware that she was there. Confident that his temperature was at a safe level, she put the pan down and sat by his side, just watching him.

Why had he told Chad Hallister that she *thrashed* him? And why let Chad believe she had sent him *poaching* for their food? She had never known Hugo to tell a deliberate lie and certainly he had never been disloyal before. What had got into him? Was it possible he had deliberately set out to make Chad Hallister feel sorry for him, thinking it the only way to make friends with the man?

Or was it simply because he needed a friend? A man to look up to; a man to confide in. Male support? Sighing, Andrea got up to walk over to Hugo's window. From here she could see the lights from the Manor. Such a big place. What would one person want with such a huge dwelling? Was Chad Hallister lonely there, living by himself, or was the Manor something he had always dreamed of having?

What was he doing now? she wondered. There were several lights burning, but he could only be in one of the rooms. Her eyes skimmed from one well-lit window to another as she tried to guess which room he would be in. Was he reading, or was he working on his latest thriller? Did he actually travel to all the exotic places in which he plotted his books, or did he get his information from other sources?

Bingo was scratching at the door. Andrea went downstairs to let him out, and Melissa followed her. 'I can't sleep,' the little girl complained. 'My throat hurts too much.'

Andrea sighed. 'Perhaps another gargling with warm salt water might help.'

With Melissa settled once more, she again found

herself by Hugo's window looking through the apple trees at the Manor. Only one light was burning now, she saw, and instinct told her Chad was in that room. A shiver raced up her spine. The way he had held her in the street—she had never reacted so strongly with any other man before.

Those eyes—how black they were! They seemed to pierce her very soul. He was undoubtedly the most attractive man she had ever known. Known? A half smile formed on her lips. She didn't know him and was never likely to know him.

Not that she would ever want to, of course! Who would, with his know-it-all attitude, his hostility, his incredible talent for jumping to conclusions! The idea—the very idea of thinking Andy McIver was a worthless drunk! Rude! He certainly was that. Had he apologised for knocking her down in the street? Of course not. Men like Chad Hallister wouldn't know the meaning of the word.

Perhaps a little of the fault lay with her, she owned reluctantly. After all, she hadn't really been watching where she was going, but then on the other hand, he was so tall, he should have seen her coming.

She continued to gaze across at the Manor, an image of his face floating in front of her, and it actually seemed as though he were there! Was she imagining it, or was somone standing at the window of the Manor? She strained her eyes to see, but of course she couldn't. It was too far, much too far, but the more she looked, the more convinced she became that someone *was* standing there and that the someone had to be Chad Hallister.

'Chad,' she softly whispered his name. 'Chad? Is that you?'

A prickly sensation swept through her body, causing her to jump back from the window and quickly draw the curtain.

Heavens! she thought. What am I doing? She drew a shaky hand to sweep back her chestnut-coloured hair and her usually soft hazel eyes had a wild look to them. Trembling, she walked over to Hugo's bedside lamp and switched it off.

She would never sleep now, she knew. She went down to the kitchen to make herself a hot chocolate.

Chad Hallister had spent the evening documenting information for his book. Alone in his upstairs den, he had got up several times to look across at the little house.

He couldn't understand why he felt so disturbed and why he found it hard to concentrate on his work. This lack of concentration had forced him to work late into the night. Suddenly, he looked up from his work and his eyes travelled to his opened window. Rubbing the stiff muscles at the back of his neck, he got up and strode over to the window.

There was only one light on at the little house now, he saw, and as he watched, he thought he saw a slender figure standing by the window. He squinted his eyes to see better, but of course he couldn't tell for sure, because it was so far away. A nerve twitched on the side of his face, but he wasn't aware of that. All he was aware of was the lovely vision of a girl's face that seemed to form in front of his eyes. The face of the girl he had given the lift to!

The slender figure faded from view and then he was looking at nothing as the light from the little house was switched off. A long, ragged sigh escaped his lips as he pushed a weary hand through his hair.

He turned to look at the papers sprawled across his desk, then decided against returning to them. It would be useless to attempt any more work tonight, he knew.

Suddenly he felt restless. Perhaps some hot chocolate spiked with brandy might help him relax.

He went down to the kitchen to make it.

CHAPTER THREE

WHEN Andrea got home from school the next afternoon, she found Chad Hallister's Rover parked in her driveway. Seeing the vehicle there made her stop in her tracks. Glancing nervously from it to the house, she wondered what would be in store for her when Chad realised that she was the dreadful Andy McIver!

She cocked her head to listen, but there weren't any sounds coming from within the house. Andrea made her way slowly to the door. With her hand on the knob, she hesitated, her heart throbbing against her ribs. Then she became angry with herself. What was she so afraid of, for goodness' sake? After all, Chad Hallister was only a man. And once he saw how joyfully the children greeted her, then he would have to know how much they all loved each other. He would probably feel ridiculous that he had believed Hugo's tales.

Andrea pushed open the door, and her hazel eyes widened in surprise. Somehow she had expected Chad and the children to be in the lounge. She hadn't expected to be immediately faced only with the presence of Chad. His huge frame was resting on one of the kitchen chairs, the chair tilted back on two legs while his feet were casually crossed *on the table*! How dared he use her kitchen table as a footstool! Slamming the door shut behind her, Andrea marched to the table.

'Get those boots off my table!' she snapped,
giving his feet a hefty shove.

He smiled lazily up at her and her heart skipped
crazily in her chest. She stepped quickly back to get
away from his disturbing closeness. His eyes trailed
down the length of her body and she could feel the
blood rushing to her cheeks. Thankful she was still
wearing her coat, she decided she wouldn't remove
it until after he left. She needed some protection
against those penetrating eyes. Even through the
thickness of her clothing, he had somehow managed to make her feel undressed.

The shove she had given his feet hadn't been
enough to remove them, but she decided against
making an issue of it. He was deliberately flaunting
his male superiority, so, like she was used to doing
with Hugo, she ignored it.

'You're home early today,' he stated casually.
'Much earlier than last evening.'

Andrea avoided his mocking glance, by busying
herself around the kitchen. Getting milk from the
fridge and chocolate from the cupboard, she next
bent down to retrieve a saucepan. 'I was able to
catch an earlier bus,' she told him, matching his
casual tone. 'When I have my car, I'm home even
earlier.' She tossed him a deliberate artificial smile,
which he had the audacity to neatly toss back with
one of his own.

'Any news about your car?' he asked, in a manner which suggested they had known each other
for years and always discussed each other's prob-
lems.

'Yes,' she answered brightly, 'it will cost a fortune for repairs, but so what?' she shrugged.

'Easy come, easy go, eh?'

'My sentiments exactly!' She whirled to face him. 'Yours, too?' she asked sweetly.

'Hardly! I work hard for my money. I make sure none of it gets wasted.'

'Like a skinflint?' she couldn't resist asking.

'No. Like a responsible person.'

Unreasonable anger flared inside her. 'Are you suggesting that I'm not?' She was facing him now, her pert little chin lifted in defiance.

Amusement lighted his eyes. Slowly he unwound his legs and got up from his chair. An angry glint replaced the laughter as he towered above her, his hands burning through her coat all the way to her flesh. Just like his eyes were burning into hers, searching for what, she did not know.

'That's exactly what I am suggesting,' he answered, his hands moving from her shoulders to the front of her coat, undoing the buttons.

'What . . . what are you doing?' she gasped, feeling the pressure of his hands against her breasts, as he slowly worked his way down her coat.

He smiled indulgently. 'Helping you off with your coat. You're indoors now, in case you haven't noticed. You'll soon be perspiring, and I detest sweaty females.'

Andrea's hands flew up to stop him, but he had already finished. She reluctantly allowed him to help her off with the coat and watched while he tossed it over the back of a chair. His eyes glanced appreciatively over the slender lines of her figure, his look resting a fraction too long on the rapid rise and fall of her breasts. Selfconsciously she smoothed down the soft wool of her red dress, a dress that she had always felt looked particularly good on her.

Feeling flustered over such a simple happening as having been helped off with her coat, she turned towards the stove. She hadn't even noticed that it had been lit. It was a job she always did herself, not trusting the children with the responsibility of lighting it, or of keeping the fire going.

Now she noticed how nice and warm the kitchen was and she was glad he had relieved her of this chore. Her eyes wandered to the woodbox. It was stacked to overflowing—another awkward chore out of the way.

She turned and her eyes swept up to his face. 'Thanks for lighting the fire and filling the woodbox,' she said gratefully, and the smile on her lips was genuine.

'Just thanks?' He smiled down at her and her heart flipped into her throat. 'No kiss? No hug?'

Andrea stepped quickly away, grabbing the saucepan to pour in the milk. The corners of her mouth lifted in a grin as she peeped at him sideways. 'Not tonight, Josephine.'

He chuckled. 'Not tonight, *Andy*?'

'I bet you feel really rotten about the things you said about me,' she laughed, stirring chocolate into the milk. 'I don't know why I didn't admit from the beginning who I was, but I guess, in a way, it was rather fascinating hearing myself described as Blackbeard the Pirate.' She looked up from the saucepan, her eyes sparkling with laughter. It all seemed rather funny now, but she was glad the charade was over. 'Did Melissa spoil Hugo's game by telling you that Andy was in fact their big sister Andrea?'

'No, I guessed that for myself,' he said softly.

'Really?' She placed the saucepan on the stove to heat the chocolate. 'I rather suspected that when I got out of the car,' she admitted, her back towards him as she stirred the drink. 'What gave it away? The fact that I was a teacher and so was Andy McIver?'

Chad came up behind her and she was aware of his presence even before he touched her. She stiffened, feeling his hands part the hair at her neck and then the thrilling sensation of his lips on the exposed skin. Gently he turned her around, an unreadable expression in his eyes as he seemed to study her face. His hands moved from her shoulders, to slide caressingly to her neck, then up to encompass her face. Her heart was caught in her throat as breathlessly she awaited his kiss.

But if it was his intention to kiss her, he was taking his time, but to Andrea, who was completely under his spell, time was of no consequence. The world stood still. She could wait for ever.

His eyes roamed leisurely from her eyes, with their misty shadows, to her mouth, softly trembling. His thumbs caressed her cheeks and then a hand slid down to cup her chin. 'You're a vision,' he said gruffly, mysteriously. 'A vision of loveliness which haunts my windowsill!' He bent his head and kissed her, his mouth moving over hers in a slowly seductive manner.

He lifted his head and again studied her as though trying to remedy a disbelief. Her lids were half closed, the thick fringe of dark lashes hiding the shadowy green-brown of her eyes. 'Last night,' he began, 'I stood by my window in my upstairs den. It was late and I was tired. There was a light on over here—an upstairs light. I thought I saw you standing at the window, and then your face seemed to float in front of me.' He smiled at the astonished look on her face as her eyes widened in wonder. 'I know,' he said, 'but crazy as it sounds, I knew then that you were Andy McIver.'

The same thing had happened to her! He released her and she had to place a hand on the chair in front of her for support. She *had* seen him by the window, then, and she *had* seen his face, just as he had seen hers!

Dazed, Andrea turned back to the stove. The chocolate was ready, but she continued to stir it absentmindedly, trying to recall articles she had read on similar phenomena. She had heard of people in love experiencing visions, but she most certainly wasn't in love with Chad Hallister and he obviously wasn't in love with her. Goodness, they hardly had exchanged a civil word between them, never mind any sweet talk! Strange, she thought. Very, very strange.

Chad had got out two cups for their hot chocolate. Andrea filled these, then reached up to the shelf to get two more, and he watched as she filled them.

'Who are they for?' he asked her.

She looked at the two cups he indicated. 'Hugo and Melissa. I probably shouldn't awaken them; they didn't get much rest last night, but I want to check how they are.'

She placed the two cups on a tray and he allowed her to get as far as the door, before he calmly announced: 'They aren't here.'

It took several seconds for his words to sink in. 'What?!'

Chad picked up his own cup and sipped at the hot beverage.

'They're over at my place. I took them there a couple of hours ago.'

Andrea stared at him, the tray still in her hands. 'Why didn't you tell me when I got home?' she demanded to know.

'You didn't ask,' he shrugged.

'Of course I didn't ask, you lout! Why would I? I thought they were here.'

'But they're not.'

'No, damn you, they're not!' She considered hurling the tray at him, but as if reading her mind, he gave her a warning glance, stood up to take the tray from her, and placed it back on the table. Picking up his cup once more, he continued sipping at it, while Andrea watched him in unconcealed disgust.

'Give me that!' she snarled, grabbing the cup from him and tipping the contents down the sink. She whirled back to face him, her eyes aglow with triumph.

'Why, you little . . .' A hand snaked out and

grabbed her wrist, pulling her towards him. His tone was menacing as he said, 'Pour me another.'

'Get it yourself!' she spat out, defiance flaring in her eyes.

His grip tightened around her wrist, hurting her, but she refused to give him the satisfaction of seeing that. He stared at her for a long moment, his black eyes locked with hers, as she glared at him. He seemed about to speak and then apparently changed his mind, freeing her wrist and rising slowly to his feet.

Andrea rubbed her wrist, watching him as he strode towards the door. Baffled that he should think of leaving before she had found out all about Hugo and Melissa, she managed to blurt out, just as he was opening the door. 'Where are you going?'

Chad turned to face her, one hand cupping the knob of the door. 'Home!' he said, his mouth twisted in a cynical curl.

'But you can't!' she protested, taking a step towards him. 'What about Hugo and Melissa?'

'What about them?' he asked her coldly.

'Well . . . well, I just can't leave them over at your place!'

'Why not? You had no qualms about leaving them alone all day in this freezing . . .' his eyes encompassed the small kitchen, looked towards the lounge, '. . . dump!'

'Dump?' she echoed. 'How dare you!' She passed a trembling hand through her thick chestnut hair, tucking some behind one pink little ear. 'We all can't live in manors, you know,' she added sarcastically.

'No, but we all can make some attempt at cleanliness,' was his caustic remark. 'This place is filthy.'

'*Filthy?*' Her eyes widened in disbelief. 'God, but you're a pompous, overbearing, arrogant . . .' she spluttered, unable to come up with anything bad enough to adequately describe this man.

He smiled, her words not affecting him in the least. When he pushed the door open to step outside, she couldn't decide which was frostier, the cold air swishing into the kitchen, or the smile on his face!

'Wait!' She hurried after him, shivering as she stepped out on to the stoop. One small hand clutched at the sleeve of his black woollen sweater, and he looked down at her hand, pale against the wool. Andrea quickly clutched her hand away, letting it drop helplessly to her side. Her eyes were softly appealing as she glanced up at his stony features. 'Please try to understand,' she begged him. 'I had to leave the children by themselves today, because I only work three days a week as it is. I can't risk losing my job, simply because the children have colds.'

It was her last six words which caused the hardness to creep back into his eyes. Roughly he grabbed her arm, steering her back into the kitchen, slamming the door shut after them.

Malevolently he said, 'All right, Andy McIver, it's time, I think, you faced up to a few home truths!' His hands were on her arms, and she felt their warmth burning through to her flesh. Bewildered by the harshness of his tone, she could only ask in a faintly puzzled voice which seemed to anger him further:

'Home truths? About me?'

He gave her a shake and she had the distinct impression he would dearly have loved to do more than just shake her.

'Yes, you little idiot. Some cold, hard facts about yourself.'

His lips hovered above hers and she seemed in danger of losing herself in the grip of smouldering black eyes. He bent his head and kissed her, his lips brutal and punishing against her own, crushing their softness until she cried out in pain. But her muffled protest only served to excite him, his arms moving around to her back, forcing her against his strong male hardness. She felt his fingers at the zipper of her dress and then his hands against the quivering skin of her exposed back.

'N-No!' she gasped, struggling violently to escape him, shivering with fear.

'Be still!' he warned, 'or so help me, you'll wish you had!' Impatiently, he unsnapped her bra and then his hand was against her breast, his thumb caressing the erected peak. She was caught in the rushing tide, like a tiny leaf, helplessly floating in the stormy, turbulent seas of sheer ecstasy. His lips devoured hers, injecting desire into every vein, igniting every sense.

Andrea didn't belong to herself any more; she belonged to Chad. Weakened by his mastery, she melted against him, and without conscience he exploited her weakness. Slipping the dress from her creamy shoulders, he sought out and kissed every

sweet curve, every vulnerable nerve, exploring
every hollow.

'Chad—no!' she gasped, tears thickening her
voice, as he slipped her dress further down her
body. Panic seized her as she sensed the madness in
his blood, the same madness which was in her own.
His hands were roaming freely now, as though he
would not be content until they had explored every
inch of her. She strained against him, unaware her
movements were highly sensual, as her body caressed his own. His hands flattened against the small of
her back, pushing her even tighter against him, his
fingers locking into the lacy edge of her panties.

Then with a suddenness that jarred her and a cry
that terrified her, he roughly put her away. Muttering something savage under his breath, he looked
down at her, saw the fear in her eyes. 'You must
have known this would happen from the minute we
set eyes on each other,' his voice rasped. 'So why
look so injured?'

Andrea couldn't speak, couldn't meet his eyes.
Quivering, she struggled to fix her dress and clasp
her bra. But her fingers were shaking, making them
clumsy, and tears of frustration, humiliation and
shame flooded her eyes, blurring her vision. Chad
grabbed her, swung her around and expertly
clasped her bra, his hands warm against her bare
skin, sending fresh tingles down her spine. She felt
her dress tighten as he zipped her up, then he
whirled her to face him and his eyes hardened at the
sight of tears flowing freely down her flushed
cheeks.

'Stop blubbering,' he commanded roughly, his

thumbs on either side of her face, smoothing away the tears.

An unreasonable anger flared within her, completely dispelling her earlier shame. She reached up and pushed his hands away, stepping backwards as she did, her eyes sparking with indignation. 'Who do you think you are, telling me what I can or cannot do?' she hissed, swiping at her cheeks to dry them. 'If I feel like c-crying, I damn well will! Anyway, that's what you were trying to do, wasn't it? Reduce me to tears for your own perverted reasons?'

He smiled lazily and she detested his smug arrogance. 'Cry?' he asked, the jeer in his voice raking against her sensitive ears. 'You were only crying because I managed to get through to that little stone in your chest other people refer to as a heart!'

Andrea gaped at him. 'What are you implying?' she demanded to know. 'That . . . that I'm *heartless*?'

He raised a quizzical brow. 'Aren't you?'

'Of course not!'

'Then how do you explain leaving two sick little children all day on their own?'

'I've told you—I must work.'

'You could have made arrangements to have someone here in your absence,' he pointed out.

'But I did. My neighbour promised to drop in and check on them occasionally.'

'Occasionally? And you really thought that was good enough?' His eyes raked her face and she flinched under his contempt.

'It was the best I could do, I keep telling you.

After all, they only have colds. Lots of people catch colds—haven't you heard, they're very common.'

'I find your flippant attitude not only distasteful, but downright irresponsible!'

She glared at him balefully and then with a sigh, sank wearily into a chair. He was right, she owned, but Chad Hallister seemed to bring out the worst in her. She peeped up at him through the thick fringe of her lashes. But what would he know of bringing up two little children on your own? The constant worry over money, the fear that not enough was being put aside for their futures. How would he know what it was like to go to work without hardly any sleep after having spent most of the night caring for them? Resentment at his unyielding attitude towards her stirred within her, but she knew it would be pointless to argue further with him.

'I do my best,' she answered simply, and suddenly she felt tired, exhaustion seeping into every bone.

'The doctor didn't seem to think you'd done your best,' he told her coldly.

'The doctor?' Her eyes had been lowered, but now they flew open, instantly alert.

'Yes, *the doctor*.' He mimicked her tone. 'He said the kids should have been seen by him much earlier. They both have bronchitis, and Hugo's is severe!'

Andrea's hand flew to her chest. 'Oh, no! Hugo got bronchitis last winter, but I didn't think this was the same.' She looked up at him helplessly, guessing at what his thoughts must be. 'His cough didn't *sound* like bronchitis,' she murmured, half apologetically. 'Th-thank you for taking them to the doctor, though. I had planned to take them myself but . . . is that why you took them? Because you guessed it was bronchitis?'

He snorted in disgust. 'I took them because I thought they had pneumonia! I came over to give them their jackets and thought I was seeing things when I saw them stretched out on the lounge floor. The place was freezing . . . no fires going, not even an electric heater to give them some comfort. They said they'd made beds down here because their bedrooms were too cold to sleep in.'

Andrea passed a weary hand through her hair. The house was cold, there was no sense denying that fact, but she did what she could to keep it warm. 'We've been having unusually cold weather this winter. Surely you don't blame me for that as well?'

'Haven't you heard of heaters? They're those contraptions that have been on the market for quite some time now. You plug them in and presto! instant heat.'

She refused to be baited. Her exhaustion was rendering her almost incapable of rational thought. 'We have a heater,' she managed to mumble, 'but the dog chewed through the wire.'

Chad studied her in silence for a few minutes, then something about her attitude caused him to ask her gently, 'Would you like to come over to the Manor and stay with them for a while?'

She shook her head. She wanted to, but she knew she couldn't. She was too tired. 'I can't,' she murmured, suddenly feeling sick.

A hardness she was lucky enough not to notice crept into his eyes. 'Can't? Or won't?' he demanded harshly.

Andrea's eyes swept to his face. 'Whatever,' she answered carelessly, too tired to care what he thought.

She heard him suck in his breath. 'Tomorrow? Do you think you'll have time for them tomorrow?'

Tomorrow was the Brownie hike. 'I have to take the Brownies on an all-day hike tomorrow,' she replied wearily.

'Brownies!' he exploded. 'What the hell are brownies?'

Andrea smiled. 'Brownies—you know, Girl Guides, Boy Scouts, Cubs. *Those* Brownies.'

'Why do you do that?' he demanded to know.

'Because Melissa is a Brownie and they needed a pack leader. I'm their leader. Melissa won't be able to go, of course, but I still must.'

'All right,' he conceded. 'That takes care of tomorrow. How about the evening? Are you free then?'

Andrea ignored the sarcasm in his voice. 'There's a barbecue planned for the parents, followed by a singalong.' She shook her head. 'It won't finish until late, I'm afraid, and Melissa and Hugo will be asleep.'

Chad bent his tall frame to lean over her. One long finger reached out to crook her chin, forcing her to look up at him. She swallowed a gulp, disturbed by his closeness, determined not to let him see it. 'That leaves us with Sunday,' he half snarled. 'Any community projects planned for Sunday, or do you think you might trouble yourself to spend a little time with your sick brother and sister?'

'I have nothing planned,' she answered calmly. 'I'll be there on Sunday.'

'Well, Halleluia!' he ejaculated. 'I'm sure they'll be thrilled!'

Andrea watched him go, bending his proud aristocratic head as he stooped to pass through her doorway. She heard him start the motor of the Range Rover and then tear out of her driveway. She knew he was angry.

After a few moments when the last sounds of Chad's vehicle had disappeared, she got up and walked slowly towards the door. Opening it, she looked out into the cold, black night.

Never had she felt so lonely. She could hardly wait for Sunday!

CHAPTER FOUR

SOME time during the night, it snowed. Andrea woke up Sunday morning to a winter wonderland. From her bedroom window she could look across at hills and valleys, their gentle slopes covered in brilliant whiteness.

Her being filled with excitement. Two nights of uninterrupted sleep had restored her usual vitality, and now she wanted nothing more than to get out into that snow and over to the Manor. The children were waiting for her and so, she hoped, was Chad! With a last lingering glance at the beauty before her, Andrea turned from her window. She had chores to do and she wanted to get started. Today promised to be perfect.

Two hours later she was ready. Dressed in a pair of warm slacks and a white woolly jumper topped with a pale blue rain-resistant jacket, Andrea stepped out into the brilliant sunny morning. A frosty wind lifted her hair, sending the chestnut curls flying and nipping at her ears. She went back into the house and after a brief search came up with a white knitted cap, which fitted snugly over her ears, the chestnut curls peeping impishly below the white rolled band.

With Bingo racing beside her, Andrea turned towards the Manor. She had only gone a few paces when suddenly she stopped. Why go the back way, across the meadow and around the pond, when she could go the front way? She was familiar with the back view of the Manor, but never had she seen it from the front. Whistling to Bingo, she turned and headed down the lane.

Their house was fairly secluded, the next dwelling being more than halfway down the lane. Andrea saw her neighbours out busily shovelling away the snow from their footpath and driveway. They exchanged hearty greetings, commented on the snow, and one neighbour informed Andrea that it had been over ten years since the last snow had fallen in the Huon Valley.

It took more than an hour for Andrea to reach the long tree-lined drive leading to the Manor, for she had stopped several times to chat briefly with friends and neighbours, each time to discuss the novelty of snow falling in the valley, and to listen to excited speculation that more was to come.

Andrea trudged up the driveway, which was lined on both sides with gigantic pine trees, their boughs leaning under the weight of snow. The sun was at an angle slanting through the treetops and where the light caught the snow, changed its colour from brilliant white to shades of purple, green and gold.

Bingo darted back and forth, stopping often to bury his little nose into the mysterious white stuff, his small tail wagging with excitement. By the time Andrea got to the top of the drive her cheeks were rosy from the frosty air and the exercise. Never had she felt more thrillingly alive!

Her heart pounded with an excitement she didn't

try to analyse when she spied Chad shovelling snow from in front of his garage. He didn't see her standing against the pine trees; a small figure blending easily into the fairy wonderland. Her eyes swept from him to view the Manor and her soft hazel eyes widened in surprise. From the back, the only view she had ever seen of the Manor, the huge dwelling had almost resembled a fortress, with its many windows and high stone walls.

But from the front, it was entirely different. Flanked by stately pines, the Manor sprawled with easy charm. Its grey stone walls were relieved by white shutters on its many windows, and below each windowsill there were white-painted flower-boxes which in summer would look beautiful with brightly coloured flowers. Geraniums, she thought.

From where Andrea stood, she could see how the Manor grounds swept down to the Huon River. Across the river were more hills and valleys, apple and pear orchards, little white houses with red painted rooftops. She turned back to Chad and her heartbeat quickened when she saw that he had noticed her. He was leaning on his shovel, dark head hatless, and even from where she stood, she could see those fierce black eyes regarding her with an intensity she was only too glad she wasn't any closer to feel.

She walked slowly towards him. 'Hullo,' she said, when she was close enough for him to hear.

'Hullo,' he returned, teeth flashing white against the dark hue of his skin. 'How was the Brownie hike yesterday?'

'Great!'

'And the barbecue afterwards?'

'Great fun. Everyone said they enjoyed it.'

Andrea realised she was gaping at him, but she couldn't help herself. He was incredibly handsome, with his jet black hair mussed from the wind, the deep colour of his skin enhancing the whiteness of perfect teeth. Dressed in a navy blue ski sweater, rolled at the neck, and in tight-fitting jeans, he was the epitome of male vitality.

Andrea dragged her eyes from his imposing form to look towards the Manor. 'How are Hugo and Melissa today?' she asked.

'Much better,' he replied in a tone which strongly suggested he didn't think she really cared about their conditions, but was merely enquiring to be polite.

'May I see them?' she asked stiffly as, ignoring her, he resumed his shovelling.

'They're asleep.'

'Asleep? Still? It's after ten o'clock!'

Chad stopped shovelling, holding the handle of the shovel with one hand as his eyes flicked casually from the little white hat on her head to the turned-down wellingtons on her feet. 'They're sick, remember?' he reminded her, and she got the feeling he thought she wasn't very bright. He was treating her as if she was a backward five-year-old! 'They awakened very early this morning—five o'clock, I think it was. They went back to sleep at nine.'

Andrea chewed on her bottom lip, fighting back the anger which threatened to spoil a glorious day. Her cheeks fused to an even darker red as he once more resumed his shovelling, breaking off neat blocks of snow, lifting and tossing them effortlessly aside.

'Well, if you could be so kind as to let me know when the next visiting hours are, I shall come back then.'

He kept her waiting for his answer until he had finished the row he was working on, then with the shovel over one shoulder he walked towards her. Bingo trotted to meet him, his little stump of a tail wagging excitedly as Chad knelt to pat him. Still patting the dog, Chad looked up at Andrea. 'The kids have missed this little fellow,' he told her. 'How about leaving him here?'

Andrea swallowed hard. 'Now?' Was he really going to send her away without even a glimpse of the sleeping children? she thought. Or was he merely suggesting it was their dog the children really missed and not herself?

'Later. When you leave.' His dark eyes mocked her. 'Or would you like a room at the Manor, too? I can assure you, there are plenty to spare.'

Braggart! she thought, her eyes sweeping towards the impressive dwelling with its many windows. 'No, thank you,' she answered primly, 'I'm rather fond of the little room I've got.' She watched him play with the dog and realised he was right. Hugo and Melissa would be feeling a bit strange, most likely, at the Manor, and perhaps the presence of their dog might be the reassuring factor they needed to help them towards a speedy recovery. 'How long do you think the children will be here?' she asked slowly, knowing it was far too cold to transport them home today.

'That depends on how long it takes them to get better,' answered Chad, still squatting beside Bingo. 'They may as well be here where they receive proper care, than with you, when you never seem to be home to look after them.'

Andrea glared down at the black hairs on his head, hating every strand. 'Very well,' she answered stiffly. 'You seem to enjoy waking up at five in the morning to the pitter-patter of little feet, and Hugo has expressed the wish to live in a manor, so why should I be the one to stand in the way of such desires and wishes?' She whirled on her heel, and when Bingo started to follow her, she sent him back. 'Stay, boy,' she commanded. 'Mr Hallister probably has something to tempt you with, too. Probably a big thick T-bone steak, much better tucker than you'd receive at *our dump*,' she added, strongly emphasising the last words as she glared balefully at Chad.

With the grace of a superbly fit athlete, Chad raised his long-limbed form and swept towards her, taking her cold fingers and warming them in his hands. 'Not so fast,' he growled. 'The kids can do without the dog. You need him for protection, I should imagine.'

'Protection?' She couldn't help but laugh. 'Protection against whom? You?'

His eyes hardened as he studied her face. 'Burglars.'

'You've got to be joking?' Andrea quipped. 'The Huon isn't New York, London or Paris! We don't have burglars *here*. Until you came, we didn't even have kidnappers!'

He laughed at that and, still holding her hands, pulled her towards him, bending his head to plant a kiss on her pert little nose. 'Enough of this ridiculous sparring,' he said softly, his warm breath fanning her cheek. 'Let's build a snowman!'

Andrea gaped up at him, stunned by his suggestion and his quick change of mood. 'A snowman?!' she repeated, amusement starting in the depths of her eyes. 'Do you know how?'

'Of course,' he grinned. 'I've built plenty . . . in New York, London and Paris!'

'I've never built any,' she admitted, an excited grin spreading across her face, 'but I've always wanted to.'

'Then let's get to it,' he smiled, his eyes lingering on the almost childish curve of her mouth and the eager expectation that shone from her eyes. 'We'll build it over there,' he suggested, indicating a point close to the wide open verandah which ran along the length of the house. 'The kids will be able to see it from their bedroom windows.'

'It's a pity they can't help us,' said Andrea, looking up at him as she walked by his side, a small hand neatly tucked into his own large one. 'They'll be terribly disappointed,' she continued, starting to feel dreadful that she should be about to enjoy the sport of building a snowman, while they were ill in bed.

'Disappointment builds character, as my mother used to say. I heard on the radio this morning that we'll be getting more of the stuff, so there should be plenty around when the kids are better,' said Chad, meeting her glance and responding with a squeeze of her hand. 'For now, they can feast their eyes on ours and then we'll do the same to theirs.'

Andrea's deep-throated chuckle brought an approving nod. 'I like to hear you laugh. On a day like today it reminds me of sleigh bells.'

'Is that a compliment, sir?'

'It is!' His arm circled her shoulders, drawing her near. 'I'm glad you came over so early,' he told her. 'I was waiting for you.'

'You were?' She slowed down and he stopped, looking down at her.

'What's wrong?' he asked, a black brow arched inquisitively.

'Well-ll, it's just that you seemed so unwelcoming earlier that I find it hard to believe you were looking *forward* to my visit. I thought you must be . . . well,' she searched for an adequate word, 'annoyed, or something.'

'I *was* annoyed,' he agreed with her, once more putting his arm around her, guiding her along. 'I was dying to get started on my snowman. I was afraid the snow would be melted before you got here to help.'

Her eyes crinkled with amusement and she playfully hit his arm. 'I'll never believe that in a thousand years,' she laughed. 'Anyway, what could I possibly do to help? You're the expert, remember? I've never even seen snow before, never mind build anything with it!'

They had arrived at the place where the snowman was to be built, and Chad made a clearing with his foot. 'I'll get you some gloves,' he told her as he took the verandah stairs three at a time, leaving

Andrea dazed and marvelling at his good humour towards her.

Perhaps it's the snow, she thought, kicking up bits of it with her toe. The snow is a novelty, and in a way, so are the children. It probably was fun for a bachelor to have a couple of kids around once in a while. But the novelty, just like the snow, would wear off and then he would get back to his books and probably forget that the McIvers ever existed.

The idea depressed her, and when Chad came out with the gloves, he noticed her change of attitude.

'What's the matter?' he asked, cupping her chin and forcing her to look up at him. 'Why the long face?'

'Oh, nothing,' she answered hastily, forcing herself to smile.

'Not getting cold, are you?' he enquired, his hand moving up to rest against her cheek. 'If you are, we can go inside. I have a fire burning in the fireplace.'

'No . . . no,' she backed away from him, wondering at his concern. 'I wouldn't miss building this snowman for the world.'

'Well, put these on,' he grinned, watching with amusement as she slid the oversized gloves on to her hands, the woollen fingers dangling crazily where her own fingers weren't long enough to fill. Impulsively, Andrea bent down and picked up a huge chunk of snow, hurtling it at Chad and catching him in the chest. Then, squealing with laughter, she raced away as he bent down to return the same. Unfortunately, Andrea turned around to see if he was coming after her, and the soft snow caught her in the face, filling her eyes and mouth.

Spluttering and laughing, she darted behind a pine tree, its bushy boughs hiding her from his view. She knew he had seen her race behind the tree, but when he didn't follow, she decided to have a peep. Presto! Caught again, only this time she didn't have a chance to clear the snow from her eyes before he was beside her and their scuffles brought them to the ground in a tangled heap.

Gasping with laughter, Andrea tried desperately to roll away from him, but he pinned her wriggling body under the weight of his own. Her eyes were bright with merriment and her clear complexion radiated health and vitality. There was a joy in her eyes that hadn't been there when he first met her.

The fun that was in her eyes was mirrored in his own. 'You little imp!' he laughed, then a look passed through his eyes that she was unable to read before it was gone, being replaced with the amused look of before. 'You're fun to be with, Andrea,' he murmured, smiling down at her. 'You're a damned good sport!'

Andrea gaped up at him. 'A good sport?' she asked weakly. Until that moment she hadn't re-alised she wanted to be more, much more than *that*!

'Mmm,' he agreed, his lips coming down on her own in a warm, friendly kiss. He raised his head to look at her and then his mouth was on hers again, only this time the softness was replaced with a sense of urgency that matched her own. His long length was completely on top of her, his arms reaching under to hold her close. Under the protection of the pine tree, with one arm still cradling her, his other came around to work its way under her clothing to cup her breast. She offered no protest, her treacherous body straining against his hand, his touch flooding her body with desire.

You're a damned good sport! His words came back, tumbling through her brain. She was a sport, all right . . . playing right into his hands. The kid next door . . . good for laughs! She struggled violently against him, his remembered words out of all proportion as they rebounded in her mind.

Chad caught her hands in one of his own, surprise registering on his face, as she continued to lash out at him.

'What's wrong?' he growled. 'You're behaving like a wildcat!'

'I . . . I don't want to be your friend!' she lashed out. 'The p-price is too high!' she added bitterly. 'Besides, I thought we were supposed to be building a snowman.'

Amusement touched his eyes. He studied her in silence for a few seconds before finally agreeing. 'You're right,' he said, rising to his feet and extending his hand to pull her up beside him. Turning her around, he neatly brushed the snow from her clothing, then without a further word strolled towards where their snowman was to be built. Andrea followed reluctantly and then watched as he made a snow ball and rolled it along the ground. She watched in amazement as the snowball quickly grew in size until it was bigger than any beachball she had ever seen. He placed it in a centre spot and then repeated the procedure. Andrea knelt, grabbed some snow, made a ball out of it and rolled it around, laughing as she struggled to move it along as it grew in size.

Chad teased her, calling her a weakling, and pretty soon they both were laughing freely and Andrea had to admit, albeit a trifle reluctantly, that she could never stay mad at Chad for long.

The ball she made was used for the head. Chad's two were used for the middle and bottom. An old hat was found in the basement of the Manor, along with a broom, a few pieces of coal and a bright red and blue scarf. While Chad was retrieving these articles, Andrea spent her time tidying up their snowman, making its waist a little trimmer, its neck not quite so squat.

After the snowman was 'dressed' and its face put on, Andrea stood beside it, her face beaming with pride. 'Isn't he handsome?' she cried, stretching up to her full height and raising her arm to pat the snowman on the head.

'You look like a snowman yourself,' Chad laughed, watching her. Her hat was almost covering her eyes and was thick with caked-on snow. The exertion of such strenuous sport had made her warm and she had long since removed her jacket, and so her jumper was in much the same state as her hat. Snow was down her boots and the fingers of her gloves had stretched even longer and tiny balls of snow hung from pulled out threads. 'Stay right where you are,' he ordered, running into the Manor and emerging a few minutes later with an extremely expensive-looking camera, the type photographers use to photograph models.

Andrea pretended she was a model, turning every which way and affecting every pose she could possibly think of, while Chad clicked away. Finally, exhausted and spent from so much laughing and posing, Andrea collapsed at the feet of the snow-man, pulling her hat off to rest her head against it. Chad took one final picture and then walked over to help her to her feet.

'C'mon, snow girl,' he said, grabbing her hat and pulling off her soggy gloves. 'When I was in getting the camera, Hannah told me the kids are awake and clamouring for a bit of attention.'

Hannah, a pleasant, middle-aged woman who was Chad's housekeeper, greeted them when they came in. She told them that the children were having their lunches and enquired whether the young lady was staying for lunch.

'Yes, but don't fix anything for us, Hannah,' Chad told her. 'We'll say hello to the kids and then I think I'll fix Miss McIver and myself some waffles in the sitting room.'

After the housekeeper had gone, disappearing along a wide corridor Chad turned to Andrea, eyeing her critically.

'You look pretty damp,' he said. 'Have you got anything on under that jumper?'

'Yes, a skivvie.' Andrea struggled out of her jumper, handing it to Chad. Gathering her hat and gloves, he looked down at her feet. They had removed their boots outside the door, but it was obvious that her socks were wet.

'Get out of those,' he said. 'I'll hand these to

Hannah, and if you look inside that bench there, you'll find some warm socks.'

While Chad carried her wet clothing to Hannah who, presumably, was going to be given the chore of getting them dry for her, Andrea searched in the bench Chad had indicated and came up with a pair of thick hockey socks. She had them on and was ready when Chad returned for her.

'How many rooms do you have here?' Andrea asked Chad, as they made their way to the children. They were walking down the corridor where Andrea had seen Hannah disappear. The hallway was extremely spacious with plenty of light coming from the several rooms on either side. Again Andrea was surprised at how cheerfully decorated the Manor was.

'Not as many as one might think,' Chad replied smilingly. 'The place gives an impression of vastness, but in truth there are only twenty or so rooms.'

'Twenty?' she echoed, astonished. 'That *many*?'

'Of course that's not counting the servants' quarters on the top floor, or the six bathrooms, or the dressing rooms,' he teased, smiling down at her wide eyed look of disbelief. 'Then there's the butler's pantry, the breakfast nook, the . . .'

'Stop! You'll make me dizzy,' she groaned. 'What made you purchase such a large place? It must cost you a fortune to heat!'

'That I couldn't tell you,' he shrugged. 'I haven't been here long enough yet to assess living costs. Most of the rooms aren't used, but will be from time to time.' He smiled down at her. 'As for buying such a large place—who knows? Perhaps some day I'll want to get married and have a half dozen children. Until that happens, let's just say I'm interested in colonial architecture and that I liked the look of the land that went with this place.'

His reference to marriage did strange things to Andrea. She peeped up at him sideways. She could easily see him with half a dozen children and loving every minute of it!

They had climbed a wide circular staircase and were continuing down another wide corridor. The bedrooms were up here. Several doors stood open. Andrea peeped in each one of them to see stately antique bedroom suites, resting on deep-piled carpeting.

'Did most of the furniture come with the place?' she asked, trusting Chad wouldn't think her too inquisitive.

'Some, but not much. Most of what I have I've collected over the years, from around the world.'

She felt like saying 'Gosh!' or 'Wow!' or something similar, but decided it would be altogether too schoolgirlish. Andrea settled for a wistful, 'It's all so beautiful! I never dreamt the Manor looked like this. From the outside, at least from the view we get, it always looked so dismal . . . so bleak and unfriendly.'

He smiled at her tone, his eyes resting on the shining lustre of her hair. 'I thought so, too,' he agreed. 'That's why I hired a team of decorators to freshen the place up a bit. They worked for over a month before I arrived.'

They had stopped at one of the doors and with his hand resting on the knob, Chad said: 'Hugo and Melissa are in here. I thought it would be less traumatic for them if they were together.'

'Yes,' Andrea agreed, grateful he had thought of this.

Hugo and Melissa were propped up in bed. A young maid was brushing Melissa's long golden tresses and one look at Hugo's curls was enough to show that he had already received the same treatment. The children's lunch trays were on a table nearby, with not a scrap of food left to be seen.

The maid, whom Chad introduced as Mary, explaining she was Hannah's niece and that she was here on a part-time basis to help out with the children, was obviously enjoying her job. Twisting Melissa's hair around her fingers, she was able to create shining ringlets on the little girls head, much to Melissa's obvious delight, who was watching the whole procedure with a hand mirror.

Andrea looked up at Chad, a grin on her face. 'Look at those little imps!' she whispered. 'They're loving every minute of this, sick or not.'

Chad nodded, watching the scene in front of him, a smile on his face. 'They've taken over the Manor, I'm afraid,' he said in low tones. 'Hannah has gone through all her recipe books searching for menus that would appeal to children. Mary spends hours reading to them and thinking up little games she thinks they might enjoy.'

Andrea looked around the room. Like the others, this room had been freshly painted and wallpapered. Her eyes rested on a bookcase, laden with brand new children's books. Next to the book-shelf was another, only this one housed several expensive-looking toys, all new. Her eyes flicked back to the children's beds. Hugo's bed was swamped with miniature cars and trucks, while a huge doll was tossed carelessly at the bottom of Melissa's bed. She looked again at Chad, who was still enjoying the spectacle of Melissa having her hair brushed.

'You don't think all this will spoil them, do you?' she asked worriedly.

Chad glanced down at her, his brows raised inquisitively. 'All what?' he asked innocently.

Andrea indicated with her arm, taking in the whole of the room, the luxury, the toys, not to mention the children's own personal maid! 'All *this*!' she repeated again.

His dark gaze mocked her. 'It's only what they deserve. There's no harm in being looked after *properly* when you're ill!'

'Of course not, but . . .' Andrea floundered for a minute, Chad's accusing look not making things any easier for her, 'but . . . but are you insinuating that I wasn't looking after them properly?' she finally whispered explosively.

'You weren't! We both know that, so why con-tinue with the issue.'

Her hazel eyes sparked with anger. 'Just because I didn't hire someone to comb their hair, clean their teeth and *read* to them, you think I wasn't looking after them properly?'

'No,' he answered firmly, his tone indicating the subject was closed, 'because you didn't get them to a doctor and because you left them to fend for themselves in a cold, damp house!'

Andrea stayed by the door while Chad strode casually towards the children. Mary had finished with Melissa's hair and the little girl was still admiring herself in the mirror, taking no notice of the young maid while she straightened blankets and fluffed up pillows. Mary gathered the trays and Andrea opened the door for her.

'Are you sure you can manage those?' Andrea asked, as Mary stepped into the hall.

'Sure. They're not heavy,' Mary assured her. 'Those sure are nice little kids you have there.'

'Thanks,' Andrea murmured, turning back to the scene in front of her. Chad had Hugo and Melissa in his arms and was standing with them at the window, showing them the snowman below. Andrea marvelled that he could hold them so easily, because they weren't, after all, babies, even though he insisted on treating them as though they were.

Watching Chad tuck them in their beds once more, Andrea felt she was the outsider. Apart from a small smile of greeting, the kids had ignored her, their attentions concentrated on all the attention they were receiving and the toys that were in front of them. Self-pity swept over her and she lavished in it for a moment, before sweeping it away. After all, she told herself, what did it really matter if she had sacrificed her life for those children, working her fingers to the bone.

Andrea walked stiffly over to them, gave them each a hug and kiss, her hand resting for a moment on each of their beautifully coiffed heads, before announcing generally, 'I must go now,' she said brightly, an unnatural light shining from her eyes. 'Everything seems to be under control here, and I just remembered I have several essays to correct and a few programmes need reviewing.'

Chad escorted her to the door. 'That was a rather sudden decision, wasn't it?' he asked. 'I invited you to lunch.'

'Sorry, but I really must go. With the children sick, I got behind in my homework.'

'They will be disappointed,' he said. 'I'm sure they expected a much longer visit from you.'

Andrea glanced over at the children. They were both submerged in puzzles. 'I'm satisfied with the care they are receiving,' she said with great dignity, 'and I'm not far away if they need me. But it is, after all, me who supports them, and to do that I must work.'

Chad didn't follow her as she made her way down the hallway, but halfway down, she turned. 'I'll leave these socks with Hannah,' she called, holding out one of her feet.

Chad laughed, walking towards her. 'Keep them,' he drawled.

'No,' she answered, 'my own will probably be dry by now.'

He came up to her. 'Those are spares I keep around for emergencies. They're warm. I want you to have them.'

It would have been foolish to argue over an old pair of socks, so Andrea reluctantly agreed. 'All right,' she murmured, looking up at him. 'I'll wear them home, but I'll return them later.'

He smiled down at her. 'Stubborn, aren't you?'

'Not usually.'

'Just today?' His eyes glinted with amusement.

Andrea realised they were no longer discussing the socks. Feeling her cheeks fuse with colour, she attempted a lighthearted laugh. 'Blame it on the snow,' she said, turning and walking the rest of the way down the corridor.

She took the back way home. Bingo raced ahead of her. At least one of us is eager to get home, she thought, watching the antics of the little dog.

Andrea wondered if Chad was watching them from an upstairs window. A prickling sensation at the back of her neck told her he might be.

He was!

CHAPTER FIVE

Iт wasn't until Chad came around the next afternoon that Andrea admitted to herself that she had
been waiting for him the whole day. Now she
wished she was wearing something far more attractive than her blue jeans and an old faded top.
Raising a hand, she quickly patted her hair in
place, tucking some wayward strands behind
her ears, before his huge frame filled her doorway. Andrea didn't greet him, or look up from her
work, but this didn't seem to deter him in the
least.

'Mmm, that smells good,' he remarked, striding
towards where she stood at the stove. 'What is it?'
he asked, peering into the bubbling pot as she
stirred with a long wooden spoon.

'Pickles,' she told him, not sparing him a glance.

'Pickles?' he echoed, in a disbelieving tone.

'Yes . . . but not like in "dill".'

He gazed at her profile. 'Are you going to tell
me, or must I guess?'

She hunched a shoulder. 'There's no big mystery
to it.'

He smiled, watching her. 'I see you want me to
guess,' he said, taking an appreciative sniff of the
bubbling brew.

She shrugged, giving him a disdainful glance.
'Why should I? It's only tomato pickles.'

He gave her a sharp look. 'You're in a prickly mood,' he said.

'I hadn't noticed, but if I am, I guess it's from chopping onions.'

Chad feigned relief. 'And here I thought it was because *I* was here!'

'Why should your presence disturb me?' she enquired sweetly.

'You seemed rather disturbed yesterday,' he reminded her.

'Oh, that,' she shrugged.

'Yes, that! You didn't seem to approve of the care the kids were receiving.'

Andrea pushed the bubbling pot to the back of the stove and looked up at him. 'That's not true. I told you I was perfectly satisfied and so, obviously, were Hugo and Melissa.'

Chad took the spoon from her and placed it on the table. Placing his hands on her shoulders, he spoke in gentle tones. 'I know it must be hard taking care of two small children, but why begrudge them a little luxury now and then?'

'What are you saying?' she gasped. 'God, you make it sound as though I'm *jealous* or something!'

'There you go again,' he said, exasperated. 'Must you misinterpret everything I do or say?'

Andrea shrugged out of his grip. With his hands on her, she found it difficult to concentrate on their discussion.

'Look,' she said, 'I haven't got time to analyse motives, words or actions. I've got work to do, even if you haven't.'

'Is that why you haven't bothered to see the

children today?' he enquired coldly. 'Because you've been so busy?'

'See for yourself!' she snapped, pointing to a row of preserves cooling on the sideboard. 'How do you think those apricots got in those jars? They certainly didn't jump in!'

'Too busy to care, eh? Is that what you want me to tell them when I get back?'

'No, just tell them *exactly* what I've been doing and they will tell you how they've been after me for weeks to get this fruit done!'

They glared at each other across the table and then Andrea whirled to the stove. Pulling the oven door open, she grabbed her oven mitts and slid out the rack. On the rack was a tray holding a dozen sterilised jars.

'Here, I'll get those,' Chad quickly offered, and she passed him the mitts which he donned and then lifting the tray, carried it to the table. 'I'll help you fill them,' he volunteered.

'I can do it myself,' she murmured. 'I wouldn't dream of wasting your time.'

'I realise you can do it yourself,' he interjected, then taking a deep breath, he smiled crookedly. 'Perhaps if I help, you might give me a taste of those pickles!'

'Oh, all right,' Andrea agreed reluctantly, but a smile touched the corners of her mouth.

'Good!' He rubbed his hands. 'You're the teacher . . . tell me what to do.'

She got him an apron which he had no qualms about wearing. Tying it around his waist, he stood in front of her, looking ridiculously absurd.

'What's the matter?' he asked, when she raised her hand to her mouth to suppress a laugh. 'Doesn't it suit me?'

Laughter bubbled through her hand. 'I don't know. Perhaps it's the colour.'

Chad looked down at the apron. 'Pink?' He grinned across at her. 'Make certain you don't tell Hugo!'

Andrea was laughing helplessly now. 'It's Hugo's apron!' she gasped. 'Melissa made it for him last Christmas. She loved the colour. I think she thought he would give it to her, but he didn't. Not that he ever wears it. That's why I gave it to you. It's the only decent-looking apron we have!'

Chad was watching her, enjoying her hilarity. 'Trying to impress me, were you?'

She wiped the tears of laughter from her eyes. 'Yes, I suppose I was. Make sure you don't get it dirty,' she warned him, and then chuckling some more, fetched ladles from the drawer.

She showed him how it was done and he watched her with interest, his dark gaze unsettling her, causing her hands to shake so much, that he finally suggested he should do it.

'You've got more on the table than in the jars,' he said, taking a ladle and filling each jar expertly.

'You've done this before,' she accused, when not so much as a drip spilled over the sides.

'No, I haven't,' he laughed. 'It's just that some people tend to be a little less clumsy than others!'

Andrea realised he was goading her, so she merely smiled at his remark. When he continued filling the jars in that same meticulous way, she couldn't resist saying, 'I bet you think I'll give you one, just because you're doing this.'

'Of course!' His glance swept over her face, amusement lighting his eyes. 'Aren't you?'

'Maybe,' she shrugged. 'Maybe not.'

His low chuckle disturbed her, its sound strangely intimate. 'Perhaps I should just take!' he taunted, and Andrea was aware of a sudden rush of blood surging through her veins.

His eyes slid down her face to rest on her mouth, and Andrea quickly bent her head so he could not see the troubled look that she knew must be in her eyes.

Why was he doing this? she wondered uneasily. She hadn't invited him to her home, but then he was the type of man who obviously didn't wait for invitations.

'All done,' he announced. 'Now where are the lids?'

Glad of the diversion, Andrea jumped from her chair to get them. 'Usually I use wax,' she explained, 'but I've run out so we'll have to use paper. The paper is waxed, so it will be all right. Here,' she said, handing him the lids, 'I'll cut out paper squares and you can screw the lids on over them. She grabbed a jar. 'I'll show you.'

Chad watched in amusement while she demonstrated, explaining how it was to be done. First she cut out a neat little square, placed it carefully over the lip of the jar and then taking one of the lids, pressed it over the paper, twisted it, and made the seal secure.

'There,' she said with satisfaction, looking across

to Chad. 'That's how it's done.' Then noticing the glitter of amusement, she asked, 'What's wrong? That's how you do it.'

'I'm sure it is,' he agreed. 'But up till now, I hadn't seen you in your role as teacher!'

Andrea laughed. 'Oh, dear,' she said. 'Is that how I sounded? Like a teacher?'

'You did,' he agreed, smilingly, 'but I liked it.'

'Well, I don't,' she confessed. 'I can't stand teachers who *sound* like teachers outside of school hours. Hugo and Melissa say living with me is like being in school twenty-four hours a day!'

'I couldn't think of anything nicer,' he murmured, but when Andrea glanced at him sharply, he had already started with one of the jars, much as if he hadn't spoken.

They worked in companionable silence for most of the time, speaking only to ask the other to pass something or another. When they had finished and cleaned up, Chad picked up one of the jars, holding it out in front of him. 'I didn't think anyone did this sort of thing any more,' he admitted, smiling ruefully. 'Home preserving . . . another lost art.'

'Not around the Huon it isn't,' Andrea disagreed. 'Practically everyone does some pickling or preserving. I'm a bit late with mine, but in the autumn you can smell it all over the village.'

'I guess the cool climate has a lot to do with it,' mused Chad, placing the jar back on the table.

'Yes, and the fact most people have woodburning stoves that are kept going most of the day. You can put a big pot on and leave it simmering at the back of your stove for hours without worrying about it. Then again, everyone has gardens. It would seem a pity not to do something with your excess produce,' she said, folding a tea-towel and putting it back on its rack. 'Are you hungry?' she asked suddenly, whirling to face him, an impish grin on her face.

'Starved!' he answered weakly, eyeing the pickles. 'I could do with a big bowl of *those*,' was his ready suggestion.

'Well, sit yourself down and I'll see if I can find something to go with them,' she said, laughing at the comical expression on his face.

After rummaging in the fridge, Andrea placed some cold brawn, butter and a bowl of the pickles on the table. Chad looked at the brawn.

'What's that?' he enquired, eyeing the meat a bit sceptically.

Andrea chuckled. 'Brawn.'

He looked from her to the meat. 'Another home-made product?'

'Yup! Boiled pig's head!'

He pushed the meat away. 'No, thanks,' he said.

'Come on, try it. It's delicious!' Andrea cut off a large piece and placed it on a plate, pushing it towards him.

'Perhaps,' he said slowly, 'if I plaster it with pickles, I just might be able to eat it.'

Andrea watched with amusement as he spooned tomato pickle over the brawn and then took a bite, chewing gingerly. He looked up at her. 'This is good,' he told her, surprised.

She flushed with pleasure. 'I thought you would like it.'

'It's better than good,' he said, taking another bite. 'It's delicious. How did you make it?'

'Well, you boil the head until all the meat falls off and then you chop the meat into small pieces. Next, you press it into a mould and . . .'

'Stop!' he commanded with a groan. 'Please! Spare me the details!'

Andrea doubled up with laughter. 'All right,' she said, 'but it's a good economical meal and good for you.' She turned to her bread basket and took out a loaf. 'I'll cut you a few slices of bread to go with it.'

When she had cut off the slices and handed them to him on a plate, he picked up a piece and examined it. 'Home-made bread!' His eyes flew to her face and he smiled at the undisguised pride he saw there. 'Did you make this as well?' he asked.

She nodded, her eyes shining.

'I can't remember the last time I had a slice of home-made bread,' he said, spreading the slice with a thick layer of butter, and chewing it with obvious enjoyment. 'I think you must be trying to impress me,' he said at last. 'Pickles, preserves, brawn and bread!'

'Just to mention a few,' she teased, 'but I don't like show-offs, so that's all you'll see today.'

She felt his eyes on her as she gathered the dishes and placed them in the sink and she couldn't help thinking how marvellous life would be if only . . . *if only she had Chad to cook for, for the rest of her life!* The idea fascinated her. She didn't really like cooking at all. But now, as she put the coffee on, she found herself wishing she had a home-made pie or cake to go with it.

They carried their coffees into the small lounge. The last of the afternoon sun had gone and the room was in shadows. Andrea put her coffee cup down and switched on the lights. Chad carried his over to the fireplace, laying it down on the mantel-shelf while he took a framed photograph down to hold in his hands. It was a family photo, taken not long before the tragic deaths of her parents and two brothers. Andrea found she was holding her breath while he studied it. He knew nothing of their circumstances and the accident was something she always found hard to talk about and she was hoping now that he would put the photograph down, and not question her about it.

Looking up from the photo, his dark gaze swept over her. She was sitting stiffly, her eyes seeming huge against the sudden paleness of her face. She shifted in her chair, avoiding his eyes. Sooner or later, the question was always put to her: Why are *you* raising your little sister and brother and not your parents? Perhaps not as bluntly as that, but in whichever way the question was put, the answer always had to be the same. Her parents were dead and so were two of her brothers.

Chad put the photograph back on the mantel-shelf and came to sit beside her on the sofa. He handed her her coffee and she accepted it with fingers that felt like matchsticks.

'Hugo and Melissa told me all about it,' he told her gently, 'and all I can say is in time you *will* work through your grief. In fact, you're doing it now, keeping yourself busy and assuming total responsibility for the kids.'

He was turned towards her, watching her and as he watched a single tear slid down her cheek. She was staring straight ahead and he saw it was the framed photograph she was looking at. Gently he removed the coffee cup from her hands as more tears followed. Her body was rigid and her teeth were clamped over her bottom lip, but still she didn't cry, the silent tears her only concession to her grief. He hadn't asked the question, but still the pain was intense. Hugo and Melissa had *told* him, had *talked* about it. She hadn't thought they *would*. She didn't know they *could*!

'Wh-when did they tell you?' she asked in a small voice.

'The day I found them in here when they were so sick.' His hand slipped beneath the chestnut curls to grasp the nape of her neck lightly. 'I saw the photograph and picked it up. They explained about the accident . . . about how you were home minding them while their parents drove their two older brothers to a basketball game . . .'

'*Stop*!' Andrea buried her face in her hands, great racking sobs shaking her body.

Chad let her cry, watching her in silence. After a long while, emotionally spent and completely exhausted, she sat beside him, wondering at what he must be thinking, but not having the heart to really care.

'Feeling better now?' he asked softly, taking a handkerchief from his pocket and gently dabbing at her cheeks.

She nodded slowly because, strangely, she did. 'We . . . never talk about . . . about what happened,' she told him, getting slowly to her feet to stand in front of the photograph. Taking it down, she pressed it to her heart, her eyes squeezed shut. Chad went over and stood beside her, his arm supporting her, holding her against him. She looked up at him. 'I . . . I'm *afraid* to talk about Mum and Dad and . . . and the boys to Hugo and Melissa,' she slowly confessed. 'I thought it would be keeping the wounds opened . . . not letting them heal, but I can see now I was wrong. They spoke to *you* about it . . . told you everything! I guess I thought because they never spoke about the accident, it didn't hurt them any more. Those first few weeks,' she went on, her head against his chest, finding comfort in the strong beat of his heart, 'were horrible! When I look back, it still seems like a dreadful nightmare.'

Chad gently took the photo from her and placed it back on the mantelshelf. Together they looked at it. 'We were such a happy family,' Andrea murmured wistfully. 'Dad and Mum adored each other. They were so proud when Wade and Geoff made the basketball team.' She smiled. 'Look at Hugo and Melissa both of them missing teeth!'

'Who's this?' asked Chad, pointing to herself in the photo.

Her smile deepened. 'You know right darn well who *that* is, it's me! Gosh, I was skinny.'

'You still are!' he grinned wickedly, his arm tightening around his waist, but she ignored the remark, meant in fun.

'This is the first time I've ever been able to stand in front of this photograph and *smile*,' she said, her eyes sweeping up to his face. 'It feels good,' she added simply.

Together they walked back to the sofa. 'Would you like some more coffee?' she asked. 'I'm afraid we've allowed it to get cold.'

'No, I've had enough,' he said, pulling her down to sit on his knee. 'Besides, I don't want you leaving me to go to the kitchen. We still have things to discuss,' he added, his lips against her cheek.

'Like what?' she asked, pushing herself away from him, so she could see his face.'

'Well, for a start, I want you to leave the kids with me for at least a couple of weeks.'

'A *couple* of weeks!' A small frown marred the smooth line of her brow. 'I don't know, Chad,' she began slowly. 'It might be too much for them. I wouldn't want them to think I've desserted them or . . . or anything.'

'All kids love a holiday from home,' he persisted. 'They need a change and so do you. Of course they'd know you hadn't deserted them, so don't use that as an excuse.'

'An excuse?' She considered this. Did she depend on the children far more than they depended on her? 'What do you mean?' she asked.

'You know perfectly well what I mean,' he drawled, watching her. 'Kids need to experience what it's like to be away from home. They need to learn how to handle themselves, away from the usual protective eye of parents or a big sister. Probably next year they'll want to go away to camp, but they won't feel free to leave you, if you make them feel guilty by going.'

'Guilty? You don't know what you're talking about,' she scoffed.

'Oh yes, I do,' his low voice was challenging. 'And so do you.'

'No, I don't!' she insisted, jumping from his lap to stand before him, hands on hips in a defiant gesture. 'Give me a for instance.'

'All right,' he drawled, leaning back against the sofa with his hands behind his head. 'How about the time Hugo was invited to go on a weekend camping trip with his friend's family? You refused permission.'

'How did you know about that?' she asked, flabbergasted.

'Hugo told me.'

'Well, did he tell you the reason *why* I refused permission?'

Chad nodded. 'He did. Hugo told me he wet the bed and that's why you said no.'

Andrea's cheeks flooded with colour. 'He told you *that*? He actually told you *that*?'

'Sure! Why not? Lots of kids his age have a similar problem. There's certainly nothing to be ashamed about. You're a teacher. It surprises me you made an issue over it.'

'I didn't make an issue over it—Hugo did that himself. He was ashamed to go. He was terrified he would have an accident and that his friend would find out and tell everyone at school. One minute he was going and the next minute he wasn't. He drove Melissa and me crazy, packing and unpacking his bag. Finally I told him he couldn't go.'

'You shouldn't have done that,' Chad rebuked

her. 'You should have let him go. Chances were that he wouldn't have wet the bed, and then he would have had something to be proud about . . . an achievement.'

Andrea flopped down on the sofa. 'I know,' she sighed, drawing up her knees to rest her chin against them. 'But I felt sorry for him. I knew he wanted me to say he couldn't go . . . to save his pride, I suppose. Anyway,' she peeped across at Chad, 'he doesn't wet the bed any more, in case you're worrying.'

He smiled. 'I know—he told me.'

Andrea returned the smile. 'But did Hugo actually . . . well, insinuate that I made them feel guilty if they went away?'

Chad's arm stretched across the top of the sofa and his hand was stroking her neck, sending delicious shivers throughout her body. 'They asked me if they could stay for a month . . .'

'A *month*?' Andrea interrupted, laughing. 'Why, those little monkeys! Of all the nerve!'

Chad's laughter mingled with hers. 'Yes, they're not backward in coming forward! When I reminded them they had a sister at home who might not agree with such a long visit, they carried on like a couple of magpies!'

'I can imagine it,' she chuckled.

'Well, they said you never let them go anywhere, or do anything.' Chad smiled, his fingers coursing through her hair. 'They said you were frightened to stay by yourself and always wanted to go wherever they went. They wanted to know if *you* could come over and stay the month with them!'

Colour flooded Andrea's cheeks. 'Oh, they did, did they?' She couldn't meet Chad's glance, but she was very much aware of those black eyes on her. 'I . . . I hope you said something suitable to put them in their place,' she murmured selfconsciously, thinking how she would dearly have loved to wring their necks!

'Oh, I did,' he assured her warmly, his hand caressing a very hot cheek. 'I told them it was a brilliant suggestion and one which I'd pondered myself!'

Her eyes flew to his face. 'What!' she gasped. Surely he was joking. Wasn't he?

'Think of it, Andrea,' he coaxed. 'The kids are already over there, and you saw for yourself how large the place is. It doesn't make sense . . . you here, the children there.'

'They could always come back.' She stated the obvious.

Chad shook his head. 'They're both much brighter, yes, but a couple of days in this damp place would soon have them back to where they were.'

'It was good enough for them before,' she muttered.

'No, it wasn't. You've already admitted Hugo had the same bout of bronchitis last winter.' He leaned towards her, a long finger reaching out to tilt her chin, forcing her to look at him. 'Give yourself a break,' he said, 'Come back to the manor with me . . . tonight!'

She felt helpless under his penetrating gaze. It was all she could do to shake her head, a weak gesture, but a refusal all the same. Chad's jaw tightened, the muscles rigid.

'Why?' he growled.

Andrea faltered under the question, which she knew to be a challenge. Her green-brown eyes made a silent appeal for understanding.

His black gaze narrowed on that look. 'Surely you don't prefer *this* place to mine?' he asked incredulously.

It was just the sort of remark she expected from him, and it was his arrogance which gave her the strength to push herself away. 'I'm not a child,' she lashed out. 'You can't dangle sweets in front of my eyes to get me to do your bidding!'

He seemed astonished by her outburst, his brows raised inquisitively. 'What are you talking about?' He ground out the words angrily, watching her. 'I daresay you know yourself!'

Andrea hunched her shoulders miserably. 'It's easy to see how you've won Hugo and Melissa,' she told him. 'What child wouldn't be delighted with all those books and toys, not to mention room service? They probably think they're in Disneyland, or some other fantasy world.' She lifted her eyes to his face. 'But I outgrew toys ages ago and I've never wanted to visit Disneyland. I don't think you . . . or your precious Manor . . . have much to offer *me*,' she added. I prefer reality to fantasy.'

'You smug little bitch!' he snarled, grabbing her shoulders and shaking her. 'Why don't you just admit you're *afraid* to spend a month at the Manor?'

'Afraid?' she asked, her lips trembling. 'Don't be

ridiculous! Why would I be afraid?'

A low groan escaped his lips. 'You mean you don't know?' He grabbed her roughly to him, his mouth only inches from hers. 'Then perhaps it's time I showed you!'

Too late she guessed his intentions. A cry of protest died in her throat, strangled, as his mouth crushed down on hers. She fought desperately to escape him, frightened by his anger and the sheer ruthlessness of his kiss. His arms encircled her, pinning her against the sofa, making any resistance not only impossible but dangerous. He tightened his grip, squeezing out her breath.

She forced herself to lie still, terrified by his brutality. Chad raised his head to look at her and then smiled down at her. 'Now you're learning,' he mocked her.

Then his mouth was on hers again, urging coaxing, inviting her to respond. And respond she did—at first hesitant and unsure, but as his hands moved over her, it gained momentum until she became his willing slave instead of his passive victim.

Her hands moved across his back, her fingers digging into the soft fleece of his sweater. She gloried in the movements of his body against hers as he pushed her deeper into the cushions of the sofa, completely covering her now with his body. His mouth left hers to nuzzle against the soft skin of her neck, to explore the sweet curves and hollows.

Then, muttering impatiently, he manoeuvred her to pull off her top and tear away her bra. 'God, but you're beautiful,' he murmured, his hands stroking the creamy smoothness of her rounded breasts. Slowly his mouth came down and Andrea gave in to exquisite ecstasy as his tongue moved over the erected peak of her nipple, before he took it into his mouth.

Desire rushed over her in torrents. Her hands cradled his head and she moaned as his mouth moved from one rosy peak to the other, his hands never stopping their exploration of her supple young body. She felt him tug at the waistband of her jeans and she wriggled her hips to help him with their removal.

Her body was on fire. It didn't belong to her any more. This was what she had been created for . . . for love. Her eyes were smoky with passion as she gazed up at Chad, watching while he removed his clothing. He smiled down at her and his eyes told her he was her master. He knelt beside her and she raised a hand to stroke the silky hairs resting on the deep tan of his well-muscled chest.

Then he was beside her again, his long length moving to completely cover the creamy smoothness of her own. His lips sought and found hers, crushing their softness, devouring them as though they were the sweetest of all honeys. She strained against him, knowing what was to surely follow, but totally powerless to resist it. His hands continued their exploration, hands that knew where to touch, to caress, to make a woman totally submissive. Inexperienced as she was, she was no match against his mastery.

Moaning with pleasure, Andrea moved her head from side to side, her eyes heavy-lidded, swollen with passion. As she turned her head once more, a corner of her eye picked up the photograph on the mantelshelf. Sanity returned with a rush and, with it, deep-rooted shame—a shame so intense that her voice was choked with a grievous disgust, as she frantically fought to push him away from her.

'Stop!' she cried desperately. 'Oh, for God's sake, please, please stop!'

He rolled off her. He had tasted her response, had found her body not only desirable but willing enough. His anger, cold and sinister, was visible in the black scowl of his face. 'Now what?' he growled impatiently, reaching for her once again. 'You picked a lousy time to have a tantrum!'

But she had the break she needed. Slipping from him, she slid off the sofa, her arms crossed to hide her breasts. She was shivering. The place was freezing. Never had she felt so *miserable*!

Chad watched her, anger such as she had never seen on a human being before clearly visible on his face. For a few desperate seconds Andrea thought he was going to lunge at her, and she knew if he did, there would be no chance of another escape. She didn't dare move; instinct told her if she did, the devil that had been released in him would strike!

Then, with what she realised was an almost superhuman effort, he gained control of himself. His shoulders shook violently and then slumped. Relieved, Andrea back away, too shattered herself to even think of running, or of grabbing her clothing which lay in a rumpled heap on the floor.

His eyes raked her body insolently, reminding her of her almost total nakedness. She darted a quick look at her clothes and he smiled sneeringly as he bent to pick them up.

'Here,' he said in a menacing voice. 'I wouldn't try this little trick too often, if I were you. It wouldn't make you very popular with your boy-friends!'

'I . . . don't have any boy-friends,' she muttered, as he tossed her clothes at her.

'I can't say I'm surprised!' he returned with a curl of his lip.

He rose slowly to his feet, slipping into his sweater as he did so. Buckling his belt, he looked across at her, standing with her clothes in her hands, still too shocked to move.

'Unless you're given to staring vacantly, I suggest you dress yourself.'

Colour rushed to her cheeks, relieving them of their paleness. 'I . . . I wasn't staring at *you*, if that's what you think,' she blurted, realising she had been.

His smile was coldly cynical. 'Well, if it's within your limited powers to dress yourself, I suggest you do so. You wouldn't want more than just your heart to freeze!'

The cutting insult was just what she needed to spur her into action. Turning her back on him, she quickly slipped her top over her head and then pulled on her jeans.

'What about this?' Chad's voice close to her ear asked, and she spun around to find him holding her bra, the flimsy, lacy garment dangling from his hand. His eyes slid to her chest, the firm young breasts obviously needing no support. He draped the garment around her neck and crossed it, as if to strangle her.

Summoning up all her courage, Andrea managed a wan kind of smile. 'You keep it,' she told him. 'A small reminder, a token if you will, that Chad Hallister can't have *everything* he wants!'

He twisted the bra tighter, but she didn't flinch or move a muscle. 'Don't fool yourself, Andrea,' he growled. 'You wanted me every bit as much as I wanted you.'

'I didn't!' she lied bravely. 'You forced me!'

'Perhaps a little at the beginning,' he was big enough to own, 'but then you came on like a powerhouse.'

How crude he made it all sound! She bowed her head in shame, knowing he had spoken the truth.

'Well, don't think it will happen again,' she answered firmly, even though her whole body was trembling, 'because it won't.'

He released the bra and it fell to the floor, limp and lifeless, a tiny scrap of material which looked strangely pathetic and vulnerable between their feet.

'Don't worry,' he said. 'A man would have to be desperate to try anything with you.'

'And of course you could never be so desperate,' she returned, her eyes flashing sparks of green.

'Never!' he agreed, then walked with long, impatient strides towards the kitchen door. Andrea took a few steps after him, his name on her lips to call him back, but when the door slammed none too gently, she halted in her tracks, her body flinching.

Slowly she turned to the photograph, then went

over and picked it up. Her mother's smiling face looked back at her and the eyes she remembered so well, were kind and understanding.

'Oh, Mom!' she whispered passionately. 'If only I could talk to you! I love him, Mom, I love him so much, but I don't know how to handle him or what I should do.'

It was a long time before she put the photo back, and when she switched off the light, her face was wet with tears.

CHAPTER SIX

TUESDAY was always a busy day for Andrea. Because she worked Wednesdays, Thursdays and Fridays, it meant Tuesdays were spent doing all the little things which would make the following three days easier.

Usually she liked to have a casserole sitting in the freezer part of the fridge, some cookies baked, the house as clean and tidy as possible and all the washing and ironing caught up with. This particular Tuesday was no exception, but she couldn't tackle her jobs with her usual enthusiasm.

She had barely slept the night before. After Chad had left and she had finally got herself to bed, she found she couldn't put him from her mind. It seemed every word he had ever spoken to her came back to haunt her. Every word, every gesture, every kiss! Her body had ached with desire and she had marvelled that she could still feel his body against hers, his arms holding her close, the feel of his mouth against her quivering flesh.

Tossing and turning, she had lain awake, and when the roosters began crowing, their calls being picked up by other roosters nearby, Andrea finally drifted off into a restless slumber. When she awoke she faced the truth that she had avoided the whole of the night. She was hopelessly in love with a man who wanted nothing more from her than a physical relationship.

Resident mistress! How could he have been so blatantly nonchalant about his offer? she wondered furiously. How dared he think she would even consider such a thing, and in front of the children too! Not to mention the housekeeper and her niece, or the people of the village. Obviously Chad Hallister didn't care whom he hurt in his quest to get what he wanted. And what did he want? The answer to that was all too painfully clear. He wanted a plaything, a cheap diversion in between books.

'I bet he could hardly believe his luck!' she muttered aloud, as she filled a bucket with hot soapy water to wash the kitchen floor. 'A helpless female alone with two little kids. I'll bet he thought all he would have to do was stand on his doorstep and whistle and we'd all come running!'

She dipped her mop into the bucket of water and then wrung it out, passing the mop around the floor in quick, angry movements. By the time the floor was washed and rinsed, the vacuuming and the dusting done, the beds changed and the washing ready to hang out, her anger had gone full circle. Now she only blamed herself. She was behaving as if she were a Victorian innocent, totally unaware of the facts of life.

She understood about body chemistry and how a man and a woman could be wildly attracted to each other. Chad only had to *look* at her and it was enough to send her pulses racing. If she didn't believe so strongly in love and marriage, then it would be easy to enter into the kind of relationship Chad had offered her.

A month! Did he feel the physical attraction they held for one another would burn out in just one month? Andrea had never had an affair before, and now she found herself wondering if a month was usually par for the course. How awful, she thought, to be cast aside like a used pair of socks. If she didn't feel so strongly about Chad, then perhaps she could be persuaded to enter into an affair. It certainly would be exciting, having Chad as a lover. Her heartbeat quickened and she felt the heat passing through her body. But she didn't want to be loved by him for just one month. A lifetime, yes, but anything short of that would kill her, she knew. To be patted on the head and sent home after a brief encounter seemed sordid, demoralising, and she knew she just wasn't worldly enough to handle it.

Therefore there was only one solution. She must let him know in no uncertain terms that she, Andrea McIver, was not up for grabs. He would have to find his lover elsewhere. That hurt! She flinched at the thought. Images of Chad holding another woman in his arms seemed evil, cruel.

Perhaps . . . perhaps if she *did* become his mistress, he might learn to love her. And she wouldn't really be his mistress, for goodness' sake. Lots of men and women made love before they married. But they would most likely be engaged, Andrea, a voice inside her said. They would have already proclaimed their undying love for one another, the voice continued. Chad doesn't love you, he only wants to use you! And you would hate being used, Andrea, you know you would!

Yes, she would hate that all right, she thought, picking up her laundry basket to carry outside. The snow had disappeared, only scant traces left as a reminder, on the high hills. It seemed an eternity had passed since she and Chad had built that snowman.

Andrea was halfway through pegging the clothes on the line when Chad drove her car into the driveway. Speechless, she could only stare at him as he swung his long frame from her little Morris.

'Well,' he drawled, walking towards her in long easy strides, 'short of a new motor, your car is practically as good as new.'

'How did you get my car from the garage?' she asked tersely.

'I drove it,' he answered innocently.

Andrea whirled on him. 'Don't be silly! You know perfectly well what I mean. It's my car and I'd planned to pick it up when I was good and ready.'

'And when would that have been?'

She shrugged. 'I told you . . . when I was ready.'

'It's been there for quite some time now. You can't expect a garage to hold it for ever, you know.'

Andrea bent down and picked up an article of clothing. Pinning it to the line, she muttered, 'I know, but . . . I was stalling for time, if you must know.'

'Why? You need it for work.'

'Of course I need it for work,' she answered patiently, 'but I also needed the money before I could take it from the garage. I get paid this week and I was going to see if they would accept instalments, but now they'll probably want the full amount.'

'Well, you needn't worry about that any longer,' he told her cheerfully. 'The account has been paid in full.'

It took several seconds for this news to sink in, and when it finally did, Andrea was furious. 'You mean . . . *you* paid for it?'

'I did,' his eyes gleamed down at her, 'but don't worry, I think I know you well enough not to expect any thanks.' The strong line of his mouth slanted into a lazy smile.

'How dare you?' she fumed, her hands forming two tiny fists at her sides. 'The whole village of Franklin will be gossiping about us soon! It's bad enough the children are over at the Manor, without you going around town paying my bills!'

Black brows rose mockingly. 'And that worries you?'

'Of course it does,' she declared bitterly. 'Hugo, Melissa and I have to live here, you know. The children go to school here. We don't want people pointing a finger at us and sniggering behind our backs. It's all right for you,' she went on, her voice rasping angrily, all the hurt and bitterness pouring out, 'you can hide behind the Manor walls, and you probably wouldn't care what people said about you *anyway*.'

'Which I wouldn't and you shouldn't either.' A faint smile crossed his lips. 'In fact, little Miss Andy McIver, I daresay you have your priorities misplaced.'

'Not likely! A teacher must guard her reputation and also the reputation of two innocent children placed in her care.'

Chad was standing directly in front of her, legs slightly apart as he gazed down at her. A coldness had crept into his eyes that chilled her, making her extremely unsure of herself. It was she who had the right to look so angry, certainly not him.

'And you think preserving your reputation is more important than safety?'

'Of course not,' she answered, wondering what he was getting at. 'I never said that.'

'But that's what you mean, isn't it?' His black eyes scorned her. 'Why else would you drive around in a car which was totally unsafe?'

Her eyes skipped over to the little Morris. 'Why else do you think it was in the garage,' she mimicked sarcastically, her eyes gloating with triumph, 'if not to have it fixed?'

'I saw the work sheet,' he continued, as if she hadn't spoken. 'The mechanic told me he'd pointed out several things which were way overdue, but which you ignored.'

'What things?'

'Bald tyres for one. Faulty brakes for another.'

Her cheeks reddened. 'Well, I admit the car has a few faults, but . . .'

'A few faults?' Chad exploded. 'God, woman, are you daft? Those are *major* faults, and you shrug them off!'

'Those are new tyres I had put on only six months ago,' she told him, walking stiffly towards her car.

'Just look at them,' she pointed out, 'they still look brand new.'

'They *are* brand new, you little idiot! I've just spent three hundred dollars getting them on.'

'Oh!' she said in a tight voice, her eyes sweeping up to his face. 'But why did you do that?'

'Saints preserve us!' he muttered, looking at her as if she were an extremely dull five-year-old. 'The old tyres were bald.'

'They weren't,' she answered crossly. 'I told you, they were only six months old.'

'Retreads. They certainly weren't new . . . not even six months ago.'

'Retreads are supposed to be like new,' she countered. 'They should certainly last longer than six months.'

'Perhaps they might have, if your wheel alignment hadn't been way off. It's a miracle you were able to steer the thing!'

Silence yawned between them as they glared at each other.

Finally Andrea spoke. 'Did the mechanic tell you why it wouldn't start?' she asked quietly.

'Yes, he did. The carburettor was loose and sucking in air which ruined the spark plugs and prevented the pistons from firing.'

'Oh,' she said, nodding wisely, 'I thought it might have been something like that.'

Chad smiled and relief flooded her body. 'You did, eh?' He reached out a hand to lay it against her cheek. 'How about if we take it for a test drive to see if everything is running smoothly?'

She gazed helplessly up at him. 'I wish you hadn't

done it,' she sighed. 'How will I ever manage to pay you back?'

His smile deepened. 'I could suggest a way, but something tells me you wouldn't like it.'

Andrea lowered her eyes, her stomach muscles tightening at his all too obvious meaning.

'Well, how about it? Shall we take a test drive?' he asked again.

She dug the toe of her shoe into the soft winter grass. 'I . . . don't think I have time,' she answered unconvincingly. 'I still have work to do, and then I'd planned to go over to see the children later and . . .'

'You couldn't have too much work with the kids away from home.' He looked across at the clothes line. 'All the clothes are hung up and the kids are quite happy watching cartoons on their television set.' His smile was charming, and Andrea felt her resolves weakening.

'Well-ll, maybe I have time for a short drive,' she agreed with a slow smile. 'Where would you like to go?'

'I thought perhaps down to Dover. We could have a late lunch there.'

It sounded wonderful. 'Fine,' she said, a smile dimpling her cheeks. 'But if we're to stop for lunch, I'd better change into something a little more glamorous than these jeans.'

'You're fine the way you are,' Chad told her, his eyes running appreciatively over the pale pink jumper and the maroon-coloured jeans.

'I'll get my jacket,' she said breathlessly, picking up the laundry basket and dashing into the house.

Once inside, she raced to the bathroom mirror and quickly brushed her hair, touched up her lipstick and then studied the results. A rosy-cheeked girl with shining brown eyes looked back at her. A date, she told her reflection. He's asked you on a date!

With her jacket slung over her arm and her bag hanging from a shoulder, Andrea ran out to meet him by the car. Chad was kneeling and patting Bingo, the little dog almost beside himself with joy.

When they got into the Morris Bingo started whining, his little tail wagging furiously at the same time.

'Do you want to bring him?' asked Chad.

'No, he gets car-sick. I really don't know why he's putting up such a fuss. He hates the car.'

But when Chad backed the car out of the driveway, Bingo ran over to the step, lifting a paw to cover his eyes.

'Look, Chad. Isn't that cute? Hugo taught him that.' Andrea's eyes swept up to his face to see if he appreciated Bingo's trick. Chad's eyes were alight with amusement as he watched Bingo, then he turned his eyes on her. 'More than cute,' he told her, and she blushed furiously because they both knew he was referring to herself.

The first part of the drive was spent in silence, Chad obviously concerned with listening to the car's motor. Finally satisfied that all was as it should be, Andrea sensed him relax and therefore was able to relax herself, enjoying the passing scenery. The twisting, curving road took them through Geeveston with its quaint little shops, and Chad

slowed down to point out an antique shop where he
had bought a butter churn.

'A butter churn!' laughed Andrea. 'What are you
going to do with it?'

They had passed out of the town and were wind-
ing their way through apple and pear orchards, the
neat rows blocked out in checkerboard patterns.

'Make butter,' he stated the obvious. 'With all
these orchards, I figured you'd probably get around
to making some homemade apple jelly, and when
you do, I want to be ready with my butter!'

She laughed gaily, her eyes sparkling with happi-
ness. 'Well, it just so happens I make excellent
apple jelly, if Melissa's and Hugo's comments are
anything to go by,' she confessed.

'Modest little thing, aren't you?' his black eyes
were gently teasing.

'Yup!' she laughed. 'Would you believe I
couldn't do any of those things until I moved to
Tasmania? This climate,' she continued, 'it's so
invigorating, it seems to call out to you to do
something, to participate with nature.' She peeped
up at him, shy suddenly. 'I guess that's why it's
sometimes called Adventure Island or even Trea-
sure Island.'

Chad smiled. 'Yes, I know what you mean,' he
agreed, and suddenly she felt very close to him.
'I'm told that in spring, it's very much like England's countryside,' he said.

'I've never been to Europe, but yes, so people
say. The hawthorn flowers in the spring, just like it
does in England, and we have the same sweetbriar
hedges,' she told him.

He glanced at her sideways, a smile curving the handsome line of his mouth. 'And are there fields of yellow daffodils?' he asked her.

'Oh, yes!' she assured him. 'Fields and fields of them, all dancing and nodding their bright yellow heads. And Chad,' she continued, her eyes glowing, 'just wait until you see the orchards in bloom! It's truly magnificent. The trees are smothered in blossom and the fragrance is out of this world.'

Parts of the road where the sun didn't get much of a chance to shine had dark patches of ice. As they drove slowly down the brown curving road they were able to see much more than if they were driving quickly.

'Is that a king fern?' Chad asked.

Andrea turned her head to look. 'Yes, beautiful, isn't it? They're very rare, you know. It's similar to the New Zealand tree-ferns, but ours have a thin, hard trunk, unlike the fibrous trunks of the more common variety.' She strained her neck, watching until the gigantic feathery fronds were lost from view. 'We were very lucky to see that,' she said. 'Usually the king fern only grows west of here, in forests along the slopes of the Hartz mountains.'

He smiled at her enthusiasm. 'Something tells me you really like this place.'

'Oh, I do,' she replied, leaning back and drinking in the fresh winter air. 'It doesn't matter where you are in Tasmania, the scenery is always beautiful. Just look at that sky! Where else in the world is a sky so blue?'

Chad's smile broadened, and when Andrea looked across at him, her heart leapt to her throat

and she forced herself to look away because she
knew it would be all too apparent in her eyes how
she felt about him.

Chad parked the car in front of a small inn at
Dover and then taking her hand strolled to the edge
of the D'Entrecasteaux Channel. Across the Channel lay the 'double' island of Bruny, clearly visible.
In the narrow neck of sand connecting North and
South Bruny, fairy penguins nested, and on the
small islands off South Bruny were muttonbird
rookeries.

'Have you ever smelled a muttonbird cooking?'
Andrea asked, her eyes dancing with mischief.

'No, what's it like?' he asked, leaving go of her
hand to drape his arm around her shoulders.

'Cod-liver oil!' Her nose wrinkled at the memory. 'The smell stays in your house for days. It's
revolting!' she chuckled.

'What's it taste like? Like it smells?'

'That I couldn't tell you,' she looked up at him
with a grin. 'After putting up with the smell of it
cooking, neither the children nor I would touch it.
Melissa and I made Hugo bury it, but that was only
after we promised to pay him a dollar . . . in
advance!'

Chad's short bark of laughter swept over her.
She had never known him to be so relaxed. 'Re-
mind me never to try some, then,' he said, smiling
down at her upturned face.

'You never know, you might like it. Most people
do . . . if you can get past the smell, of course!'

His arm tightened around her and he dropped his
head to kiss her lightly on the mouth. 'No, thanks. I

think I'll take your word for it. I hated cod-liver oil
as a kid.'

'Me too,' she murmured happily, thrilled by the
touch of his kiss. He gathered her closer until the
soft chestnut curls were fanned against his shoulder. 'Do . . . do you like scallops?' she asked,
almost shyly.

'Love them!' he told her, his lips pressed against
her hair.

'Well, the Channel contains Tasmania's main
scallop beds,' she said breathlessly, as his mouth
moved down to gently nuzzle her ear.

'Does it?' he asked, and she had the impression
he didn't much care as his mouth moved slowly
across her cheek to seek out her mouth. As if in a
dream she raised her face, her lips parted to receive
his kiss. His mouth was gently persuasive at first,
his lips moving across hers in slow caressing movements. Then he turned her towards him, his arms
encircling her like tight bands of steel, his mouth
bearing down on hers with an urgent pressure. She
felt her arms move up, her hands coursing through
the thick scrub of his hair, and she returned his kiss
with an urgency that was as great as his own.

Finally he released her, his eyes raking her
face. 'I'm sorry, Andrea,' he muttered hoarsely.
'After last night, I didn't mean for this to happen
again.'

She could only nod, her eyes lowered. She didn't
trust herself to speak. Finally she dragged her eyes
up to meet his. 'I'm . . . sorry too,' she whispered,
wondering if he knew she was lying.

They walked back to the inn in uneasy silence—

a silence so oppressive that Andrea felt choked by it. How could a kiss destroy the beauty of a perfect day? she wondered, daring to risk a glance at Chad's stony features. She had to practically run to keep pace with him, and several times she even wondered if he was trying to shake her off.

But doggedly she kept up with him and when they finally reached the inn she was without breath. 'Let's not bother with lunch,' she panted, thinking she would only gag on anything put in front of her if she was forced to eat in such disagreeable company.

A brief smile curved his mouth as he looked down at her, taking in the tossled curls, the flushed cheeks and the rapid heaving of her chest.

'We'll have lunch,' he said curtly, placing his hand on the small of her back and propelling her into the inn.

The inn was dark and with only a few patrons. A log fire was blazing in a open stone fireplace at one end of the room, and as Chad guided her towards it, Andrea felt a thrill of pride as people glanced curiously at them. Even dressed casually in jeans and what seemed to be his favourite black sweater, Chad was an interesting study of male virility combined with an elegance which caught and held the eye. It never occurred to her that her own gentle beauty had anything to do with the curiosity they were arousing as they took their seats at one of the small rounded tables.

The menu was chalked on to a blackboard and although the selection was limited to only a few dishes, each one sounded delicious. Andrea studied the selection, her eyes riveted to the board in order to avoid glancing at Chad.

'Well,' he drawled at last, 'what will you have?'

His voice made her start. 'I . . . I don't know,' she answered slowly, her eyes never leaving the menu. 'It's so hard to choose.' She hunched her shoulders forward, presumably to get a better view of the selection.

'There are only *three* dishes,' he pointed out. 'Surely you can decide on one.'

'Well, that's just it,' she answered. 'The choice is so limited . . . it makes it hard to choose.' She risked a sideway glance. 'What are you having?'

'Tasmania is noted for its crayfish,' he shrugged, 'so I thought I would have the crayfish salad.'

'Then that's what I'll have,' she decided.

But just as Chad got up to place their orders at the counter, the cook sauntered from the kitchen and brushed the 'Crayfish Salad' off the board. ''All out of crayfish!' he announced generally, beaming broadly.

Somehow Andrea managed to suppress her laughter, as she once again turned to study the menu. 'Well, that narrows the field considerably,' she observed, still choking back her laughter.

'Suppose you take one and I'll take the other?' Chad suggested, and Andrea shot him a look, hearing the hint of laughter in his voice.

'All right,' she laughed aloud, grateful not to have to contain it any longer. 'Scallops for me.'

'King Neptune's platter for me.'

'We'll share,' she suggested hopefully.

'Like hell!' he growled smilingly, getting up once again to place their orders, this time successfully.

The meal was delicious and they ate with healthy appetites. Chad reluctantly allowed Andrea to sample two of his oysters which he made her pay back with two of her scallops. Helped along with the wine they chose to have with their meal, the earlier tension disappeared and conversation was lighthearted and warm. Finally Chad glanced at his watch and whistled. 'We'll have to go,' he announced. 'I must be back by three.'

They drove most of the way back in companionable silence, their conversation mostly circling around the black swans they happened to see swimming in the river.

'Aren't they graceful?' Andrea enthused. 'Quick, Chad, look!' she pointed excitedly. 'Their young! I never knew baby swans were called cygnets until we moved to Tasmania. The town of Cygnet is named after them.'

Chad merely smiled at her enthusiasm and because he seemed rather preoccupied, Andrea remained silent until they stopped at the bottom of the Manor drive.

'I'll get out here,' Chad turned to her and said. 'I think you'll find the car working perfectly now, but if I don't see you until tomorrow, drive carefully to work.'

Andrea watched as he slid his long frame from the car, and then she took her place behind the wheel, nibbling at her bottom lip in confusion and disappointment. She had expected him to invite her back to the Manor to visit Hugo and Melissa, but now it seemed as if he wanted to get rid of her.

'Are you sure you don't want a lift up?' she enquired hopefully.

'No, there's still a fair bit of snow on the drive-way. The trees block out most of the sun, so it hasn't melted. Those little wheels of yours might get bogged down.'

'Oh, all right,' she answered in a small voice. 'Thanks for lunch and for the car . . . and everything.'

'My pleasure,' he said, smiling as he turned to walk up the drive.

She watched him go and then went herself. But once at home, she decided she had misinterpreted his reluctance to have her at the Manor. There was no reason why he should object to her visiting the children, so he must have thought she was tired, or still had more housework to do.

After all, she had told him earlier that she had work to do. Her eyes rested on a neat pile of underthings she had placed on the kitchen table to take over to the children. She would take them over now, she decided, along with some fresh vegetables. A smile spread slowly over her face. Hadn't she promised Chad she would pay him back for Hugo's jacket with turnips and carrots?

A quick rummage through her cold pantry produced several lovely bunches of long tapering carrots; a few turnips not many, because she remembered he didn't like turnips and some choice beetroot.

Placing the vegetables in a basket and the clothing in a brown paper bag, Andrea set off for the Manor with Bingo racing ahead of her. They went the back way, through the apple trees and across the meadow, skirting the edge of the pond and on up until they came to the front of the Manor.

The snowman, surprisingly, was still intact but Andrea saw that its hat and long red and blue scarf were missing. Giving it an affectionate pat on the head, she turned and ran up the steps leading to the verandah.

After taking the largest bunch of carrots from the basket, she held them high overhead before she reached out to ring the door bell. After several rings, the huge oak door was finally opened and Chad stood in front of her, staring in astonishment at the carrots she held dangling over her head.

'Who is it, Chad darling?' a feminine voice sang out from behind. Chad turned to smile at the girl who came to stand beside him, her arm circling his in a possessive manner as she gazed curiously at Andrea still holding the carrots.

Chad turned back to Andrea, his black eyes glittering with amusement. Andrea appeared as if she had suddenly been turned into a statue as she gaped at the beautiful blonde standing next to Chad. Incredibly, the only thing that registered in her brain was that the blonde was wearing the snowman's hat and that she also had his scarf draped around her neck. Her numbed brain refused to admit that apparently she had Chad as well!

It wasn't until the blonde laughed and asked Chad again who she was that Andrea finally re-

alised how ridiculous she must look standing there
with her carrots.

'This is Andy McIver,' she heard Chad say.
'Andy McIver . . . the carrot lady!'

CHAPTER SEVEN

HER training as a teacher saved her. Dropping the carrots into the basket, Andrea smiled brightly at the blonde whom Chad introduced as Sherri West, a 'friend' visiting from Sydney.

'How do you do,' Andrea murmured politely, feeling the colour rise in her cheeks. The blonde she faced was tall and slender, and she met Andrea's fiery, embarrassed gaze with a thin, frigid smile. Seeing her standing close beside Chad with her arm still tucked in his, Andrea couldn't help but wonder what their relationship was, or how deeply it ran.

The blonde was perfectly dressed in an elegant suit of powdery blue wool which seemed to match her eyes to perfection. Even the snowman's scarf draped across her shoulders blended in with the outfit. Sherri West's thin, angular face was carefully made up and she looked to Andrea as if she had just stepped off the pages of a fashion magazine. But there was a certain coldly artificial element in the woman's image of perfection that left Andrea with a strange chill.

Chad had changed out of his jeans and black sweater into a pair of neat fitting grey slacks. His navy silk shirt, stretched tautly over the muscles of his chest and unbuttoned at the neck, seemed to blend in with Sherri's outfit, his rugged dark looks highlighting the girl's fairness.

Compared to them Andrea felt like a poor rela-
tion, dressed as she still was in her maroon jeans
and pink sweater.

'Let's see what else you have in here,' Chad
laughed openly, bending to pick up the basket and
carrying it inside. His face was alight with amusement, and Andrea would have given anything at
that moment to effectively wipe that mocking grin
from his face.

'There's not much else, really,' Andrea muttered, following him inside, wishing he wouldn't
insist going through the basket with Sherri watching on. Somehow she didn't feel Sherri would be
particularly interested in home-grown vegetables.

Chad sorted through the basket holding up for
close inspection the several bunches of carrots, the
beetroot and the turnips.

Turning to Sherri, he asked her. 'Do you like
turnips?'

Sherri wrinkled her nose in distaste, and visibly
shuddered. 'Now, Chad,' she drawled, 'you know
perfectly well what vegetables I like, and *turnips*
certainly isn't amongst them. I've never known you
to like them either.'

The turnips had been included as a joke, a private joke between herself and Chad, but now
Andrea found herself wishing she had never
brought them. In fact she was fervently wishing she
had stayed at home and not come around to the
Manor in the first place. But at least she now knew
why Chad had been in such a hurry to get home and
why he hadn't invited her in after their drive.

Obviously he had invited Sherri to the Manor as his guest and he didn't want the embarrassment of herself around.

Chad turned to Andrea and shot her a grin. 'Perhaps it's time I learned to like them,' he said. 'They might go nicely with muttonbird!'

Andrea flushed at this veiled reminder of their drive and a quick glance at Sherri's narrowed eyes was enough to convince her that it hadn't gone unnoticed by the girl.

'I'll take these out to the kitchen,' said Chad, holding the basket. 'Hannah might want them for dinner tonight.'

'Oh, I'll take them,' Andrea offered quickly, reaching for the basket, but Chad held it away from her.

'You and Sherri can go into the sitting room, get acquainted with each other,' he told them, his eyes slightly taunting.

After he had gone Sherri turned to Andrea. 'If you would rather go home I can explain to Chad that you had to leave.' Her eyes travelled down Andrea's jean-clad form. 'He wasn't expecting you, anyway.'

What Sherri really meant was: he wasn't expecting you, *so why did you come?* At least, thought Andrea, that was what her tone of voice said.

'No, I realise he wasn't, but I had a few things to bring over to my little sister and brother,' Andrea explained, wondering if Sherri knew about Hugo and Melissa.

Sherri eyed her curiously. 'Yes, I've met them,' she said, reaching up to untwine the scarf from around her shoulders. Tossing it and the hat carelessly on the bench, she added thoughtfully, 'Perhaps Chad's suggestion that we get to know each other wasn't such a bad one after all. Let's go into the sitting room. I have a glass of wine going in there.'

Andrea followed her into the sitting room, a beautifully decorated room with bright prints and cosy furnishings. The last of the afternoon sun was streaming through plate glass windows and Andrea saw that logs were sitting in the open fireplace waiting to be lit.

Sherri walked over to the windows and drew the curtains, blocking out the sun. 'I can't stand sun in my eyes,' she explained, as she crossed over to pick up her drink from a silver tray. Settling herself in one of the overstuffed chairs, she viewed Andrea from the rim of her glass.

Sherri didn't invite Andrea to take a seat, nor did she bother offering her a glass of wine, but that didn't bother Andrea. She didn't want any wine, the wine she had consumed at lunch was quite sufficient for the day. Automatically, she went over to stand in front of the fireplace, a habit she had assumed during winters in Tasmania. Lit or not!

'It's too early for a fire,' Sherri commented. 'Chad got it ready to light later this evening. We both enjoy sitting around a fire with the lights turned low. Do you?'

'Yes,' Andrea agreed, and she couldn't help adding, 'It's so romantic!'

Sherri glanced at her sharply, trying to guess at

her meaning. 'I presume you have a boy-friend?' she asked.

Andrea shook her head. 'Not at the moment.'

'What do you think of Chad?' Sherri asked unexpectedly.

'I don't know him very well,' Andrea shrugged, evading the question rather effectively, she thought.

'But you know him well enough to allow him full responsibility for the children,' Sherri was quick to point out.

'Yes—well, as far as neighbours go, he must be one of the best,' Andrea explained.

'And one of the richest?' Her gaze was jeering, pointed.

'Meaning?' Andrea asked tautly.

'Oh, come now, sweetie, don't play coy with me,' Sherri laughed archly, and took a sip of her wine. 'It's obvious what your game is, and if Chad can't see through it now, he will in time.'

'I don't know what you're talking about,' Andrea frowned.

'Sure you do,' Sherri purred. 'You're using those kids upstairs to get at Chad!'

'*What!*' Andrea gasped.

Another tinkling laugh and Sherri jibed, 'What I find amazing is how you think a plain little mouse like yourself could possibly hold any appeal to a man like Chad. Really, darling, you're way out of your class!'

Andrea eyed her with distaste, both for the person and the cruel implication. 'But you're not, obviously.'

Sherri gave a luxurious stretch, the blue eyes narrowed to glittering slits. 'See for yourself darling. There's hardly a comparison!'

'A comparison to what?' Chad's voice from the doorway drawled, and both women snapped their heads around to view Chad lounging against the frame, a tray of biscuits and cheese in his hands. As he strode casually across the room to place the tray next to the one holding the decanter of wine, Andrea could tell by his composure that he had only heard Sherri's last comment. But Sherri, obviously, was not so sure. The transformation in the woman was nothing short of miraculous, and had Andrea not been the victim of her rude comments, she might have found the swift change in character amusing.

Tucking away her sharp claws, Sherri immediately became a playful kitten. Jumping up from her chair she hurried over to Chad, squealing with delight over the assortment of cheeses.

'Oh, Chad,' she gushed, clapping her hands like a small child. 'Gouda—my *favourite!*' The smile she gave Chad and the manner in which her eyes were wide with unaffected innocence sickened Andrea, and when Chad sliced off a bit of the cheese and put it on a cracker, handing it to her with an affectionate smile of his own, Andrea felt sure she was going to be sick.

'Another?' asked Chad, when Sherri had finished what surely must have been a gastronomic delight, if the 'ooohs' and 'aahs' and 'mms' were anything to go by!

'Oh, please,' she cooed, and when Chad bent his

head to slice off the cheese, Sherri shot Andrea a triumphant smirk.

See, darling? her look told Andrea. He hasn't paid you the slightest amount of attention. And why would he when he's got *me* to cater to!

Chad handed Sherri the cheese and then turned to Andrea. 'What would you like?' he asked.

'Nothing for me, thanks,' she replied stiffly.

'You're sure?' His brows quirked inquisitively and she saw amusement dance briefly in his eyes. 'I thought a sharp Cheddar would be to your liking.'

If he was making reference to her sharp tongue, Andrea wasn't amused. 'No, thank you,' she answered politely once more.

For the first time Chad noticed she was without a glass of wine. Turning abruptly to Sherri, he asked, 'Didn't you offer Andrea a glass of wine?' There was an underlying tinge of coldness to his voice.

'Of course I did, darling,' Sherri lied openly. 'Several times, as a matter of fact, but I'm afraid she must enjoy being difficult. Either that or she's watching her weight. *Short* people do have to be careful, you know, Chad,' she continued, looking up at him with wide innocent eyes, before smiling benevolently at Andrea. 'I have a friend about your height, and she's constantly on guard against unwanted bumps and bulges.'

Chad's deep-throated chuckle did nothing to soothe Andrea's rapidly growing temper, nor did his comment.

'Andrea's bumps and bulges are certainly well placed at the present.' His eyes slid rakishly down the slender line of her body.

If Andrea's face couldn't get any redder it certainly was becoming hotter. Sherri's shrewd eyes fastened on Andrea's flushed cheeks, and anger sparkled in her blue eyes at Chad's words, which were all too obviously a compliment.

Andrea moved away from the fireplace, feeling like a piece of meat displayed in a butcher shop. 'I've never considered five feet seven inches to be exactly short,' she remarked, unconsciously holding her head up high.

'Of course it's not,' Sherri surprised Andrea by saying. 'It must be those jeans and that bulky sweater which give the illusion of shortness . . . a sort of boxy appearance.'

Andrea smiled at her. 'Thanks,' she muttered, catching and holding her eyes. 'I'll remember that!' she added pointedly. Turning to Chad, she said, 'Perhaps wine and cheese another time, but it's getting late and I still haven't seen the children.' She smiled at them both. 'It's been lovely,' she said. 'Really!' she added, in case there might be some doubt.

'Not so fast,' laughed Chad, catching her arm. 'Hannah thanks you for the vegetables and has suggested you stay for dinner.' He glanced at his watch. 'Dinner won't be for at least an hour, so that gives you plenty of time with the children.'

Before Andrea had a chance to answer, Sherri cut in. 'That Hannah!' she sighed painfully. 'She must be a glutton for punishment. Really, Chad, had I known poor Hannah had the extra burden of those children to care for, I never would have consented to this visit. But even overworked as she so obviously must be, she still finds it in her heart to invite another for dinner.' She shook her head sadly. 'I don't know how she copes, Chad, I honestly don't!'

Chad smiled down at her upturned face and put his arm around her shoulder. 'Don't worry about it, sweetie,' he told her in a softly soothing voice. 'Hannah is a real trouper. Besides, she's got her young niece to help her over any rough patches.'

'I know,' Sherri sighed, leaning her golden head against his shoulder. 'It's silly of me to worry, but with so many people for her to cook and clean for, it does make me feel as though I could have chosen a better time to come.'

He hugged her closer. 'Any time would be the best time for you, my sweet!' Turning to Andrea, he repeated the invitation.

'No, thank you. Sherri's quite right, it wouldn't be fair to Hannah,' she told him, not missing the gloating look from Sherri as she nestled against Chad's arm.

Unwrapping himself from his blonde sweetheart, he accompanied Andrea to the door. 'What's wrong?' he asked, following her into the corridor. 'You know perfectly well Hannah wouldn't mind having you stay for dinner.'

Hannah wouldn't, but Sherri certainly would! Andrea couldn't believe Chad could be so blind. But then love *was* blind, she thought. Or so people said.

'No, it's all right.' She couldn't meet his eyes. Instead she studied the pattern on the rug. 'I've got work to do tonight. Papers to correct . . . that sort of thing.'

'Andrea—look at me!'

Confused by his tone, Andrea could only do as he said. Dragging her eyes miserably to his face, she wasn't aware of the single tear that rolled forlornly down the curve of her cheek. 'Yes?' she asked softly.

'What's wrong?' he asked gently, wiping away the tear with the back of his hand. 'Why are you crying?'

'I'm not,' she sniffed, attempting to move away from him. His touch was more than she could bear.

'Something's wrong,' he frowned, not letting her go, his hands firmly on her shoulders. 'And unless you tell me what . . .'

'Chad!' Sherri's demanding voice interrupted. 'Chad darling, what's keeping you?'

Andrea and Chad turned towards Sherri standing in the doorway. Her beautiful features were turned into a carefully studied pout, causing Andrea to wonder if the girl had practised it in a mirror.

Chad dropped his hands from Andrea's shoulders. 'I'll be with you in a minute, Sherri,' he drawled impatiently. 'Pour yourself a glass of wine, there's a good girl.'

'But Chad,' she said, going towards him and Andrea and placing one of her carefully manicured hands on his arm, 'it's getting chilly in there. I think you should light the fire.'

'Soon!' he growled, and this time Sherri had the good sense to do what he said. Casting Andrea a spiteful glance, she backed away and went into the sitting room. Chad turned his attention once more to Andrea.

'Sherri's not the reason for your—er—shall we say, discomfort?' he asked smilingly.

'Of course not,' she lied bravely, and even managed a smile to help prove it.

'That's good,' he said, returning the smile. 'Because I'm sure once you two get to know each other, you'll become good friends.'

Andrea couldn't imagine that happening in a thousand years, but felt it wise to keep this knowledge to herself.

'You'd better go,' she said instead. 'It does get cold once the sun goes down, and I'd better get up to see Hugo and Melissa.'

He studied her thoughtfully for a few seconds. 'I'll go with you,' he told her quietly.

'No!' He had taken her arm and now she wrenched it free, surprising him with the suddenness of her action. 'No,' she said again, this time a little more calmly. 'I . . . I haven't seen them alone for a while now,' she attempted to explain, 'and . . . and I might not get to see them for the rest of this week, with work and everything . . .' Her voice trailed off and once more she couldn't meet his eyes, her toe tracing the now familiar pattern of the carpeting. How could she tell him she was afraid Sherri would follow them upstairs and she didn't think she could bear watching him pay any more attention to the girl?

'All right,' he said gruffly, after a while. 'I can understand your need for a private visit.'

He seemed about to touch her, his hand reaching out . . . and then abruptly, as if he had suddenly thought better of it, he thrust his hands into his pockets. Then with a movement that was almost savage, he turned and entered the sitting room, the door closing firmly after him.

Andrea stood staring at the beautiful sheen of the cedar door. Through its thickness she could hear the deep rumbling tones of her beloved Chad's voice, followed by the strident laughter of his mysterious and beautiful house guest.

Miserably, she turned and followed the corridor to the large entrance hall where she had left her bag containing the children's clothing. As she picked it up, her eyes fastened on the snowman's scarf. Had Chad told Sherri, she wondered, that *she* had helped build that snowman?

The lights had been turned on now that dusk had arrived and the Manor took on a charm that was both elegant and peaceful, the soft lighting enhancing the gleaming pieces of rosewood furniture that dotted the corridor. Andrea checked in at the kitchen before going up to see the children. She decided she had better tell Hannah that she wouldn't be staying for dinner before that good lady went to any extra trouble.

The kitchen was, and with every conceivable contraption designed to lessen the housewife's burden was at Hannah's fingertips. The housekeeper looked up when Andrea entered and gave her a warm smile.

'It was very thoughtful of you,' she said, 'to bring those vegetables to us. Our garden hasn't been planted yet, so fresh vegetables are a real treat.'

Andrea felt warmed by the kindly words and she almost wished she could stay for dinner. Not to eat with Chad and Sherri, but to stay here in this comfortable and roomy kitchen with its delicious smells and pleasant company. She sighed, thinking of the lonely meal she would have at home in her dreary kitchen with only Bingo as company.

'I won't be staying for dinner, Hannah,' she said wistfully, looking around at the copper pots and pans lining the brown brick wall behind the huge stove. Hannah looked up from the pavlova she was preparing and eyed her critically.

'Why ever not?' she asked sharply. 'By the look of you, you could do with a good hot meal.'

Andrea smiled, but shook her head. 'It smells delicious,' she said, her nostrils twitching appreciatively. 'Is that roast beef?'

'It is,' Hannah chuckled. 'Roast beef, Yorkshire pudding, roast potatoes, thick gravy and plenty of vegetables, yours included.'

'Oh, you haven't cooked the turnips, I hope? Chad—I mean Mr Hallister—detests turnips!'

'Does he now? Well, it so happens he told me to make certain I cooked them. Now, doesn't that beat all?'

'Yes,' Andrea agreed, avoiding Hannah's amused glance.

'Then there's cherry pie and pavlova for dessert,' the housekeeper continued, wiping her hands on her apron. 'Now are you going to eat better than that at your home tonight?'

Andrea thought of the canned soup she would most likely be having. 'Not likely!'

'I didn't think so,' Hannah glowered. 'You young people, you're all the same. I don't know,' she muttered, 'beats me how most of you survive.' She looked across at Andrea, who had taken a seat at the gleaming pine table, her soft hazel eyes resting on the potted fern in the centre.

'You look tired,' Hannah commented. 'Are you feeling all right?'

Andrea looked up at the kindly face. 'I'm fine, Hannah,' she said. 'I was just admiring that leafy fern. It looks so pretty against the pine. Is it an asparagus fern?'

'It is,' Hannah smiled, obviously pleased with the attention the plant was receiving. 'I potted it myself.'

Mary, Hannah's niece, came into the kitchen, and after her initial surprise at seeing Andrea in the kitchen, she smiled shyly. 'H'lo, Miss McIver,' she said. 'I didn't know you were here. Will you be going up to see Hugo and Melissa?'

'Yes, right now,' Andrea answered, rising from the table and smiling at the girl, 'How have the little monsters been today?'

'Good as gold!' Mary laughed. 'But they're hungry and it's their tea time. I was just coming down to get their trays ready.'

'Well, it's a good thing I'm here, then,' Andrea smiled. 'I can help you carry them up.'

Hannah had already carved thick slices from the roast in readiness for the children. She took the platter containing the meat from the warmer and placed it on plates, while Mary and Andrea scooped vegetables around the thick, juicy slices.

'Hugo's eyes will pop out of his head when he sees this gravy!' Andrea laughed, as she poured plenty over the mashed potatoes.

'What are you doing in here?' Chad's angry voice boomed behind them.

Andrea whirled to face him, the ladle she was holding dripping gravy on to the floor. His eyes glittered dangerously as he glared down into her startled face. Snatching the ladle from her hand, he passed it to Hannah.

'I'm quite certain Hannah is capable of running this kitchen without any interference from you,' he rasped. 'Besides, you indicated earlier that you couldn't possibly get along for one more minute without seeing the kids. Now it appears it was a bloody lie!'

Andrea's cheeks flooded with colour. She couldn't believe Chad could speak so rudely to her in front of Hannah and Mary. Deeply embarrassed, she cast a hasty glance in the direction of the two women and found to her relief that they were discreetly tending to their duties.

She didn't resist when Chad grabbed her elbow and steered her unceremoniously across the kitchen. Pausing at the door, he turned to Hannah. 'Miss McIver couldn't be persuaded to dine with Miss West and myself. Perhaps if you fix up another tray, she'll eat with the children!' With that, he led her through the door and dragged her down the corridor.

When they were at the foot of the stairs, Andrea

snatched her arm from his grip, unconsciously rubbing where his fingers had dug into her flesh.

'How dare you speak to me like that!' she snapped. 'Don't you believe I have feelings, or that other people might?'

'Other people, yes! You? I'm not so sure.'

She raised her hand to strike him, but he grabbed her hand and pulled her towards him, and she shrank from the cruelty in his eyes.

'Don't ever try that again,' he told her in deeply sinister tones, 'because I give you fair warning, I would have no hesitation in giving the same back!'

There was no doubt in her mind that he spoke the truth, but that didn't prevent her from goading him further.

'I knew from the beginning there was something about you that warned me to be cautious,' she quipped. 'Now I know what that something was. You enjoy inflicting pain on others! You especially enjoy hurting *me*!'

'You're so right!' he snarled, his lips curled into a sneer. A hand shot out and gripped her chin, forcing her head back, and she knew her face was drained of every vestige of colour. It struck her at that moment that his anger was out of all proportion, that something or someone had provoked him into this attack. *Sherri!* Had Sherri said something to him about herself? It had to be. Surely her presence in the kitchen couldn't be sufficient to unleash such unreasonable fury in him.

She stumbled when he pushed her away from

him. The black eyes raked her cringing body with the sort of contempt that made her tremble. Then suddenly he grabbed her again, jerking her body forward and thrusting her head back until she was forced to look into the fiery depths of those fierce black eyes.

'You sicken me!' he snarled, in a voice that was like a whiplash. 'You, with your soft look of innocence. You're nothing but an opportunist . . . a money-grubbing little bitch!'

So that was it! She had guessed correctly. Sherri had wasted no time in sinking her claws in a little farther.

Andrea shook her head from side to side, not trusting herself to speak. Her silent denial only served to fan Chad's fury, and he shook her violently.

'Don't deny it.' His anger overcame him and she felt his fingers pressing against her throat. 'Admit it!' he snarled. 'Admit it, or so help me God, I'll kill you!'

She couldn't speak. Terrified, she twisted her body, trying desperately to escape his hold. 'Admit it,' he said in a soft voice, when he had withdrawn his hand.

Andrea backed away from him, her hand going to her throat. 'You're mad,' she whispered, feeling for the railing behind her for support. Her face was deathly white and her eyes were huge in the chalky paleness. She never knew what gave her the courage to say, 'Believe what you want about me, I don't really care—but before you start making false accusations check on your facts. Even the

guilty are presumed innocent until proven other-
wise!'

With that she turned and fled up the stairs, her
heart crashing painfully against her ribs.

CHAPTER EIGHT

WHEN Andrea got home that night she could barely recall her visit to Hugo and Melissa. It had taken her several minutes to regain her composure, and it was only by sheer effort that she was able to maintain some degree of normalcy for the sake of the children.

Several times they had asked her what was wrong, but each time she had replied that there was nothing the matter, it was just that she was tired, there was work tomorrow, and so on. Hannah and Mary had brought up the trays and had clucked over her sympathetically, giving her cause to wonder if she and Chad had been overheard in the corridor.

Mary brought up the bag containing the children's clothing which Andrea had left in the kitchen owing to the hasty departure she had been forced to accept. But when Andrea had taken out the various articles to place them in the children's bureau, Hugo and Melissa protested.

'We've got brand new things, Andy. We don't need those!'

It was true. The drawers were packed with frilly underthings for Melissa and shorts and shirts for Hugo. Andrea stared at the garments. There were pyjamas galore. The children had certainly been well catered for.

'Look,' Hugo had told her. 'We even have our very own colour TV—Chad got it for us.'

After Mary had taken away the trays, Andrea had slumped into a chair. She had eaten very little of her meal, but the children had gulped theirs down with a speed that fascinated Andrea.

The only part of the conversation with the children she could vividly recall was when Melissa had asked if she had met Sherri. Now, as she sat alone at her own kitchen table, the conversation came back with amazing clarity.

'Have you met Chad's girl-friend?' Melissa had asked her.

'Yes.'

'Isn't she beautiful?'

'Very.'

'Hugo doesn't think so, but then what would he know?' Melissa had scoffed.

Andrea had turned to Hugo. He was watching television and hadn't appeared interested in the conversation. But he had looked up when he heard his name mentioned.

'Sherri looks like one of Melissa's dolls,' he quipped.

'Hugo thinks Sherri is too shiny,' Melissa had added.

'She is,' Hugo had defended his observation. 'She doesn't look real like you do, Andy,' he had told her. 'You always look nice and messy!'

With that, he had turned back to his programme, leaving Andrea to stare at him, wondering if he was right.

Now she looked down at her jumper and her

jeans. She did look messy! No wonder Sherri had looked at her as if she were a grub. Andrea got up and went into the bathroom. Stripping off her clothes, she stepped into the shower. She stayed under the piercing stream until she felt cleansed, until she was certain she could no longer feel Chad's hands on her, or the sting of his words.

With Bingo fed and her clothes laid out for the next day, she went to bed. She hadn't bothered making a fire and she lay shivering under the covers until her body gradually warmed them. Were Chad and Sherri sitting in front of the fireplace she couldn't help wondering. Or worse . . . were they together in bed?

A deep knot of pain twisted in the pit of her stomach, and she recognised it for what it was: pangs of jealousy. There was no future for her with Chad, she had always known that, but now she was totally convinced. His kisses had meant nothing to him. He had only been amusing himself at her expense. It was Sherri he cared for . . . Sherri he loved.

Andrea tossed and turned, wondering what she should do. She considered taking the children away from the Manor, but then decided this would be the worst thing she could do. They still were fairly ill, and she had her job. She didn't want Chad coming around and finding them alone again. And he had been right, she was willing to admit. The house was damp and it was cold. The children would suffer a setback and then he would be stomping around accusing her of God knew what.

No, the wisest thing would be to leave them at

the Manor. With the children at the Manor and with Sherri there she needn't worry about Chad paying any unexpected visits to the house. The next two weeks were going to be busy for her. It was testing time and parents would be attending interviews. She had told Melissa and Hugo she wouldn't be seeing much of them during this period, and because they knew the routine, had understood. They had told her Chad was going to take them for a drive up the mountains to look at the snow and that in a few days, when they were that much better, he was going to take them on a snow picnic'.

Andrea lay in the darkness wondering what she should do once her hectic two weeks was over and the school holidays began. It would be difficult, if not impossible, to avoid Chad then. Should she move, perhaps try her luck at finding another place in the Huon? But that would mean a different school for the children. They wouldn't like leaving their friends. Andrea rolled over on her side. Who was she fooling? she asked herself. The children would hate leaving Chad and . . . and so would she!

Better to gobble up the few crumbs he passed her than to be without his company entirely. Damn that Sherri West and her rude and insulting comments! Andrea had no doubt that the blonde had passed her suspicions on to Chad that she was after his money. But it wasn't his money she was after, it was his love. Finally Andrea drifted off into a restless slumber.

The three days proved just as tiring as she knew they would be. Most parents couldn't attend interviews during the day, so Andrea had to conduct them in the early part of the evenings, so it was always well past nine before she arrived home, cold and exhausted.

On Thursday night she didn't get home until almost ten because she had stayed in town to do some late-night shopping. When she opened her kitchen door she saw there was a note lying on the table. Picking it up, she knew immediately from the bold scrawl that Chad had written it. The words on the single sheet of paper brought a smile to her lips.

WHERE THE HELL HAVE YOU BEEN ALL EVENING? WAITED UNTIL NINE-THIRTY. COME FOR DINNER TOMOR-ROW NIGHT. SEVEN SHARP—OR ELSE!!! CHAD.

The next morning Andrea rang the Manor from school. Had she the telephone on at home, she would have rung Chad immediately after reading the note. The note, as cryptic as it was, had thrilled her. Chad, in his own way, was letting her know that he had forgiven her for whatever it was that he had found her guilty of. She even dared hope that he had sent Sherri packing, but when the telephone was picked up and she heard Sherri's voice on the other end, her hopes were effectively squashed.

'Hello,' said Andrea. 'This is Andrea McIver. May I speak to Chad, please?'

'Who did you say it was?' Sherri's voice cooed.

'Andrea—Andrea McIver.'

'Oh! I thought that's what you said.' A pause. 'Why do you want to speak with Chad?'

It was none of Sherri's business why, and Andrea

felt like saying this, but instead she said as civilly as she could manage, 'I have a message for him.'

'Well, I'm afraid you'll have to give it to me,' Sherri answered. 'Chad's very busy. He's up in his den.'

Andrea hesitated. She didn't trust Sherri, but what else could she do? 'That's all right,' she said at last. 'I'll ring back later.'

'Won't do you any good,' Sherri snapped impatiently. 'I've told you, Chad is busy. He left explicit orders that he wasn't to be disturbed on any account.'

'Very well,' Andrea sighed. 'Please tell him, when he comes up for air, that I won't be able to come for dinner tonight because I can't get home until nine o'clock.'

'He's invited you for dinner?' Sherri's voice came over the wire in a screech. 'I don't believe you!'

'Well, sorry to disappoint you, but I'm afraid he has. You will make certain he gets the message?'

'He'll get the message all right!' Sherri promised, then Andrea was holding the phone listening to the dialling tone.

She smiled as she replaced the phone. 'So,' she said aloud, 'the big, beautiful blonde is afraid of the little brown mouse!'

The next morning Andrea did her housework and then dressed in her best slacks, pale beige flannel topped with a chocolate brown rollneck sweater. Once again she filled a basket with vegetables and with Bingo at her heels headed towards the Manor. She knew the Manor could get along without the few vegetables, but it made her feel she was at least contributing something towards the children's keep.

The Manor seemed strangely deserted when she approached the back. Usually she could hear sounds coming from the kitchen, Hannah's voice calling out to Mary or the general clinks and clangs of pots and pans rattling. Andrea knocked softly on the kitchen door and when no one came to answer, opened the door a crack and poked her head inside. Then she swung the door wider and stared in wide-eyed amazement.

The once beautiful kitchen now looked as if a cyclone had visited it. Dirty dishes were everywhere, scattered along the counters and over the long pine table. Pots held the remains of dried mashed potatoes, blackened peas and grey cauliflower. Andrea moved slowly across the kitchen, stepping over spills that had been allowed to dry on the once gleaming tiles. The dishwasher was stacked with dirty dishes, but no one had bothered to turn it on.

Hannah's asparagus fern had been pushed aside, a roasting pan containing a hunk of something black squashed against it. Andrea dragged the pan away and picked up the plant, wondering if she could save it. After a quick search she found a pair of scissors and snipped off the broken ferns, watered it and placed it on the windowsill out of reach of the general debris.

What had happened? she kept asking herself. Where was Hannah? Where was Mary? Outside in the corridor she listened for sounds. The household was absolutely still. Her eyes strayed to the antique furniture where dust was beginning to collect.

With growing anxiety she raced down the hall and then up the stairs. The children weren't in their room, nor had their beds been made. Clothing was scattered across the floor and on their table were the remains of a sloppy breakfast. Out in the passageway again, she thought she heard the faint sound of music coming from the far end of the hall. Following the sounds, but walking cautiously, for she had never been in this wing of the Manor before, she finally came across Hugo and Melissa watching television in the upstairs lounge. They turned when they heard her come in.

'Andy!' cried Melissa, getting up from where she was stretched on the floor beside Hugo. 'We've been waiting for you!' she squealed, racing towards her sister.

'Yeah!' agreed Hugo, joining Melissa to hug Andrea. 'We've been waiting for you since last night! Where have you been?'

Laughing with relief that they were all right, Andrea dragged them down to sit beside her on a brightly coloured sofa. They were both dressed and seemed in perfect shape, all traces of their bronchitis apparently gone.

'You were supposed to come for dinner last night,' Melissa pouted. 'We waited and waited!'

'I cooked the dinner,' Hugo announced. 'Roast lamb!'

'*You* cooked the dinner?' asked Andrea in astonishment, thinking of the nightmarish kitchen. 'Oh no!' she groaned.

'I cooked the dessert,' declared Melissa. 'Chocolate cake!'

'But where's Hannah?' Andrea asked. 'And Mary? Where's Chad . . . and Sherri?'

'Hannah's brother had an accident—his tractor rolled on top of him!' explained Hugo.

'Oh, no!' gasped Andrea. 'How dreadful! When did it happen?'

'Yesterday afternoon. Chad had to take Hannah and Mary to the farm. He said he might have to stay a while to help out, but that you would soon be here. We waited and waited, and in the end we just ate the cake and went to bed.'

'You mean you've been alone since yesterday afternoon? Did Sherri go to the farm too?'

'No, Sherri's here,' answered Melissa. 'At least, we *think* she's here.'

'What do you mean?'

'Well, we haven't seen her since Chad and Hannah and Mary left. She said if we wanted dinner to cook it ourselves and that we weren't to bother her.'

'Oh, she did, did she?' Andrea fumed. 'And where might she be now, I wonder?'

'In bed, most probably. Why? What's wrong with me and Hugo cooking dinner?' Melissa demanded to know.

'The mess, for one thing, and the fact you could have burned the house down for another!' Andrea stated quite firmly. 'Honestly, you two! You should have known better!'

'But we were hungry,' wailed Hugo. 'We had to eat something.'

'You could have had something cold from the fridge, so don't give me any of that nonsense.'

'We only did what we were supposed to,' blubbered Melissa, starting to cry. 'H-Hannah had everything ready, we just followed the note.'

'The note?' frowned Andrea, puzzled.

'The note Hannah left for Sherri,' supplied Hugo. 'Sherri told us not to bother her, so we put the roast on at five o'clock, the vegetables on at six-thirty and mixed up flour for gravy just as it said in the note. It was real easy!'

'You forgot the cake, Hugo,' Melissa managed to mumble between sobs. 'Don't forget I put the cake in at five-thirty!'

'Oh, yeah,' Hugo agreed, 'Melissa put the cake in at five-thirty.'

'It was specially planned for you,' whimpered Melissa pathetically. 'You were supposed to be here for seven o'clock. We didn't want you coming for dinner and then not finding any!'

'All right, all right,' Andrea soothed her. 'It's easy to see what happened, and I guess you were only trying to help.'

'But why didn't you come?' Hugo asked now. 'You haven't told us.'

'Because I was working late. I rang Chad to tell him, but he was busy, so I told Sherri. She must have forgotten to tell him. It was a mix-up all around.'

But had Sherri forgotten, Andrea wondered, or had she deliberately not told Chad that she wouldn't be coming? It all seemed so pointless, though. Sherri had nothing to gain, surely, by not passing on her message. Perhaps she really had forgotten. There must have been plenty of commotion when Hannah heard about her brother. It could have slipped her mind in all the confusion. Thank goodness nothing worse than a messy kitchen had transpired.

'I'd better get started on that kitchen,' she sighed, getting to her feet.

'Should we help?' Hugo asked coyly, 'or should we watch a little more TV?'

Andrea shut the set off. 'You and Melissa can clean your room,' she told them firmly. 'It's a mess!'

'Mary will do it when she gets back,' Hugo muttered, looking miserably at the silent television.

'Yes, and Hannah will clean the kitchen,' added Melissa, her cheerfulness restored. 'We never have to do any work here, Andy. Hannah and Mary are *servants*. They do it.'

Andrea stared at them, anger rising like a torpedo to her throat. 'Hannah and Mary are *people*,' she told them. 'They're here to help run the household, not to pick up after two little kids who are fast becoming spoilt!'

'Sherri calls them servants. We heard her tell Chad he would need more servants if he was going to take in any more peasants.' Melissa turned to her brother. 'Didn't we hear Sherri say that?'

'Yup!' Hugo grinned. 'She meant us,' he declared importantly. 'We're the peasants.'

Andrea looked at them, hardly believing her ears, her cheeks flaming with colour. How dared

Chad and Sherri discuss her brother and sister in such terms! Peasants, indeed!

'After you've finished cleaning your room,' she told them between stiff lips, 'get your things together. When I'm through with the kitchen, we're going home.'

'Home!' The children chorussed. 'But we don't want to go home! Chad said we could stay for a month, and the month isn't up yet.'

'Tough! Just do as I say!'

With that Andrea marched stiffly from the room, wondering, as she made her way down to the kitchen, how adults could possibly say such cruel things in front of two innocent children.

She had only just got on one of Hannah's over-sized aprons when Chad entered the kitchen from the back door. He looked tired, as though he had been up all night, but he seemed pleased to find Andrea there. His eyes travelled from her to the surrounding mess.

'Well,' he drawled with a grin, 'looks like you had quite a party!'

Andrea fought an urge to go to him, to help him off with his jacket, to insist he sit down and to offer him a cup of tea. But instead she turned away from him, busying herself at the sink. He came up behind her, wrapping his arms around her waist, and she closed her eyes when she felt his lips press against her cheek.

'Oh, Andrea,' he groaned, 'I've missed you these past few days!' She trembled when his lips left her cheek to nuzzle against her neck. Excited shivers raced down her spine. 'Have you missed me?' he asked softly, his hands moving up to encircle her breasts.

'No!' she gasped, wrenching his hands away and kicking his shin with the heel of her shoe at the same time.

The suddenness of her actions caught him by surprise, enabling her to move away from the sink and around to the opposite side of the long, pine table.

'I . . . I haven't forgotten what you called me the other night!' she lashed out, bitterness in her voice.

Chad swept a weary hand through the thick scrub of his hair and once more her heart went out to him, and she remembered the reason why he was tired.

'How . . . how is Hannah's brother?' she asked.

He pulled out a chair and sat down, pushing away some of the mess on the table to make way for his arms.

'It was touch and go for most of the night, but the doctors are confident he'll be as good as new in a few months.' His eyes swept over to hold hers. 'Hannah and Mary were pretty shaken up. I've given them a month off to help out with the farm and so that Hannah can comfort her sister-in-law.'

Was he telling her that he couldn't keep the children with him now that there was no one to do the fetching and carrying? Thank goodness she had already made her decision to take the children home before she had to suffer the humiliation of seeing them turfed out like . . . like *peasants*!

'That was kind of you,' she told him. And it was, she had to admit. 'Hannah will be a great comfort to her sister-in-law.'

'She will,' he agreed, his eyes leaving hers to look again around the kitchen. 'I'm glad she's not here to see this mess! I only hope I can have it cleaned up before she gets back!' he grinned, looking back at Andrea. 'Was dinner good? Hannah was worried Sherri wouldn't get it on in time and that the "poor working girl", as she likes to call you, would be kept waiting.'

Andrea didn't answer. Instead she started stacking dishes. Chad reached across and grabbed her hand, and startled, she looked at him. 'I said I was sorry, Andrea,' he said softly. 'Can't you forgive me?'

She could only look at him. What had happened to make him treat her so differently? The last time she had been with him, even his cold black looks had just about killed her.

'There's nothing to forgive,' she managed at last, relieved that her few words had been sufficient for him to drop her hand. 'Anyway, you haven't *said* you were sorry,' she huffed.

He smiled, his eyes caressing her face. 'But I've *shown* you!'

He meant the kiss, of course. How typically arrogant of him, to think a kiss could take away the stings of his insults!

'Kiss and make it better, is it?' she asked, carrying a pile of dishes over to the sink. Chad came to stand beside her and she noticed the tea-towel in his hand.

'If you want, I could do better!' he suggested roguishly.

'No, thank you,' she answered primly, pouring

powdered soap over the dishes before letting the water run on them. 'A simple "Andrea, would you please find it in your heart to forgive my unfortunate choice of words the other night, because if you would I'd be so grateful that I will, without whimper or pout, clean up this entire kitchen while you sit and watch!" would do.'

Her look was challenging as she gazed up at his amused face. 'Well?' she asked, a delightful smile dimpling her cheeks. 'What say you?'

His laughter warmed her, going straight to her heart. 'I say I would do anything to see you smile like that just one more time,' he told her, his eyes on her mouth.

She turned quickly away, confusion darkening her eyes. What was she doing, laughing and joking with him when only minutes ago Hugo and Melissa had told her Chad had allowed Sherri to refer to them as peasants? She dipped a plate into the sudsy water and placed it on the draining-board, returning her hand to the sink to retrieve another. His dark hand closed over hers, taking it from the water to dry it on his tea-towel.

'I want to be forgiven,' he said, and although his eyes were still glittering with amusement she knew he was being serious. 'Please, sweet Andrea—sit and watch!'

Her smile was slow in forming. 'No, I want to help.' Then she said the words she had been wanting to say. 'You look tired. Are you hungry? I'll put the kettle on and make you some tea.'

Without warning he grabbed her to him, his arms like tight bands of steel as they imprisoned her against him. 'Oh, Andrea,' he groaned, 'I meant it when I said I've missed you. Last night . . . well, I can only say that throughout it all I found comfort knowing you were safe at the Manor. My only regret was that I wasn't here with you.' He released her sufficiently to smile down at her face. 'I was hoping you would still be here when I got back.'

'How touching!' Sherri's shrill voice shrieked from behind.

Chad released Andrea and they both turned towards Sherri. She wad dressed in a pale pink satin robe, her long blonde hair draped across her shoulders. Even with very little make-up she was stunningly beautiful.

Sherri marched over to the sink and before anyone could guess her intentions, she raised her hand and slapped Andrea's face. 'You little tramp!' she snapped furiously, raising her arm to strike again, only this time Chad grabbed her and steered her to a chair.

Andrea watched in startled disbelief as he tended to Sherri as if she had been the one struck. Gingerly, Andrea raised shaking fingers to her cheek. She could feel the raised imprint of Sherri's hand.

Andrea watched helplessly as Chad held Sherri in his arms while the girl wept copious tears. Finally he led her out of the kitchen, and Andrea could hear Sherri's sobs mingling with Chad's soothing voice as they made their way down the corridor.

Hugo and Melissa came into the kitchen. 'What's happened to Sherri?' asked Hugo. 'Chad had to carry her upstairs.'

'Yes, and she was crying,' Melissa added.

'We've cleaned up our room, just like you told us,' Hugo informed her. 'How come you haven't finished cleaning up in here?'

'Yeah,' sighed Melissa, 'how come?'

'You talk about *us* being slow,' Hugo complained. 'You're taking forever in here!'

'You shoulda got Chad to help you,' said Melissa.

'How could Chad help her when he's got his arms loaded up with Sherri?' Hugo pointed out.

'Well, he won't be able to help now,' Melissa wagged her head. 'He's probably taken Sherri to her room, and when he goes in there he takes a long time before he comes back out!'

'That's true,' Hugo agreed. 'I wonder what they do in there?'

'Kiss, most likely,' Melissa laughed.

'Yuk! I bet they don't! Chad couldn't be bothered kissing any old girls.'

'He could too,' Melissa insisted. 'I've seen Chad kissing Sherri.'

'Bet you haven't.'

'Bet I have!'

Andrea stared at them both, her eyes going from one child to the other. Finally she put her hands up to her ears. 'Stop!' she pleaded. 'Stop!'

'What's wrong with you?' Hugo demanded to know. 'We're just talking about Chad and Sherri. What's wrong with that?'

There was nothing wrong with that—nothing at all. So neither Hugo nor Melissa could understand why Andrea sat down at the table, dropped her head on her arms and wept.

Hugo looked at Melissa and shrugged.

Melissa looked at Hugo and she shrugged.

'Both of 'em crying,' Hugo muttered. 'Wonder what Chad's done to them? Must have been a beauty, whatever it was!'

CHAPTER NINE

CHAD didn't stay 'hours' with Sherri. Within half an hour he was down in the kitchen. Andrea had the dishwasher going and the kids were busy scraping pots and pans. Both sides of the sink were lined with still more dishes, and Chad grabbed a towel to begin wiping.

Andrea looked up from the sink when she heard him enter the kitchen and then hastily looked away. She knew her eyes were most probably red and swollen from crying and she didn't want Chad noticing. But when he stood beside her to dry the dishes, she felt his eyes on her. Nervously she reached up a sudsy hand to tuck a few stray hairs behind her ears, then bent her head over the sink.

Chad put his hand on her cheek and stroked it gently. 'I'm sorry about that,' he sighed. 'Sherri hasn't been herself lately. She tells me she's coming down with a cold.'

Andrea cast him a mocking glance. 'That explains everything!' she quipped sarcastically, and then immediately regretted her words. There was nothing to be gained by putting herself on the same nasty level as Sherri. Besides, Chad had been through enough. He was tired, and she didn't envy him having the Manor to look after on his own along with the added burden of Sherri to care for. 'I hope she'll feel better by tomorrow,' she added in compensation.

With all of them working and with Chad keeping the children organised, the kitchen soon took on the appearance it undoubtedly had had when Hannah had left it. Even so, it was well into the afternoon by the time they finished, and when Chad asked if anyone was hungry, Andrea remembered she hadn't eaten since breakfast that morning. Nor had the children, although they hadn't stopped nibbling the whole time the kitchen was being restored.

Chad got out a cold ham from the fridge and began making up some thick sandwiches.

'I wonder if Sherri would like a cup of tea and a sandwich?' Andrea suggested to Chad. 'I don't think she's had anything to eat today. She must be starved.'

Chad looked at her and smiled. 'Even though she struck you, you can find it in your heart to worry about her stomach?' he quizzed.

'You said she wasn't feeling well. She won't get better if she doesn't eat.'

'True.' One dark eyebrow was raised in amusement. 'Do you want to take it up to her, or shall I?'

Andrea hesitated. Sherri would detest having her go up, but she didn't want Chad to think she was afraid of the woman. 'I'll take a tray to her,' she volunteered, going to the cupboard to get one. When she began placing items on it, Chad stopped her.

'Have your own first,' he ordered. 'You wouldn't want to face Sherri on an empty stomach, now

would you?' His eyes were gently mocking, and
Andrea laughed.

'I guess not!' she agreed.

Their snack was delicious. Chad proved to be an
excellent sandwich maker, and Andrea only had to
make the tea. Fresh fruit finished off the meal, and
Andrea got up from the table to prepare Sherri's
tray while Chad and the children cleared away the
dishes.

'Which room is Sherri's?' Andrea asked.

'Third one on the right along the landing,' Chad
told her. 'Are you sure you can manage that thing?
It's not too heavy?'

'No,' she smiled. 'Light as a feather. A sandwich
and a cup of tea don't weight a ton, you know!'

Upstairs, she tapped softly on Sherri's bedroom
door. She didn't want to wake her in case she was
sleeping.

'Come in, darling,' Sherri's voice sang out. But
when Andrea stepped inside, her tone changed
dramatically. 'Oh, it's you!' she glowered. 'What
are you still doing here? I would have thought
you'd have the good sense to go home where you
belong.'

'I'll be going soon enough,' Andrea answered
cheerfully, carrying the tray across the room.

'Domestic work suits you,' Sherri sneered. 'You
look comfortable carrying a tray.'

'Really?' Andrea smiled sweetly. 'How nice of
you to say so.'

Sherri glared at her. 'I suppose Chad made you
bring my tray up,' she sniggered cruelly. 'How
terrible for you, to be forced to wait on me!'

'Not at all,' Andrea returned. 'Chad had already been up once, I thought it only fair to spare him a second trip.'

'What!' Sherri sat up straight against her pillows. 'Spare him? How dare you! Chad would gladly crawl on his hands and knees all the way to Perth for me, if I wanted him to!'

'You like to see people crawl, don't you, Sherri? For myself, I prefer them standing straight and tall.' Andrea looked down at the tray she had placed on a coffee table. 'Would you like to eat in bed, or would you prefer eating here at the table?'

'You bitch! Get out of my room!' Sherri shouted.

Andrea shrugged. 'Very well, but you're sure you can manage all by yourself?' she asked innocently. 'You don't look at all well. Your face has gone all red,' she observed, with a concerned frown. 'Must be fever.'

'Get out!' Sherri screamed, throwing a pillow at Andrea. 'Get out, I say!'

Andrea hesitated. 'Are you *sure* you want me to leave?' she asked. 'You're not just pretending?'

'*Get out!*'

'Oh, all right,' sighed Andrea, walking slowly towards the door. 'If you insist.'

When she was safely out in the corridor, she put her hand over her mouth and doubled up in helpless laughter. Chad met her at the foot of the stairs.

'How did it go?' he asked.

'Fine.'

His eyes swept over her face and he smiled. 'It must have—you look positively radiant!'

She put her hands to her face. Her cheeks were

hot. 'Do I?' she asked. 'I guess it's because I've found a way to-er-get along with Sherri,' she said, then added, 'so to speak.'

Chad put his arm around her. 'Sherri's a bit spoilt, but basically she's a nice kid. I'm glad you two have decided to bury the hatchet.'

If Sherri had her way she would bury it in my back! Andrea thought, as she walked with Chad back to the kitchen.

'Where are the children?' she asked, looking around the big but now very clean kitchen.

'In the sitting room having a game of Scrabble.'

She should tell him now of her decision to take the children home with her, but she found she couldn't. It was still early, so she decided to let them finish their game. Instead she said, 'Bingo hasn't eaten yet. Would you mind if I gave him something to eat?'

'Of course not. He's part of the family. Feed him whatever you want.'

Andrea went over to the roast she had covered with a clean tea-towel and had left lying on the counter top, not quite knowing what should be done with it.

'What *is* that?' Chad asked, peering over her shoulder.

'Last night's roast,' she answered.

'Poor Sherri,' he chuckled. 'She's not a very good cook, I'm afraid, but at least she tried. I had some reservations about leaving her with the meal *and* the kids to look after, but Hannah wrote everything down for her. We knew you would be here at seven and Sherri promised to see you were settled in one of the bedrooms.' He stuffed his hands into his pockets and stared at the charred remains of the roast. 'Actually, I'm rather proud of how well she coped. It couldn't have been easy, considering she wasn't feeling well.' He smiled down at Andrea's upturned face. 'It must have been pleasant for you,' he said, 'to come back from work and not have to worry about cooking anything.'

Andrea nodded and looked down at the roast. He was so obviously pleased with what he thought Sherri's accomplishments were that she knew she could never find it in her heart to tell him the truth. Miserably she began hacking at the roast, hoping to find something suitable in the middle to give to Bingo. Chad took the knife from her hand.

'You're not thinking of giving Bingo that for his dinner?' he asked. 'It will make him sick.'

'I suppose you're right,' she sighed. 'I'll get him something at home.' She looked away from him, to carefully study Hannah's fern which had taken its rightful place again on the polished pine table. 'The children are better, Chad. I'm taking them home,' she said quietly.

She heard his sharp intake of breath. 'Why?'

Andrea swung her head around and lifted her eyes to his face. 'I told you—they're better. There's no need for them to stay any longer.'

His eyes narrowed dangerously. 'Is that the only reason?' he glowered.

'Of course! What other reason could there be?'

'You promised them a month.' His face had gone white, the lines of it harsh and bitter, and in his eyes she could see the terrifying violence she had seen in them a few times before. Nervously she stepped back.

'I . . . I know I did, but . . .'

Chad grabbed her arm, the pressure of his grip causing her to wince. 'But what?' he broke in, his voice harsh, savage.

'Stop it!' she gasped. 'You're hurting me!'

She stared at him and he stared back, as if he was searching for something, she did not know what.

'Answer me!' he rasped. 'There must be a good reason why you would deliberately break a promise.'

She shook her head. 'No . . . it's just as I said . . .'

His breathing was ragged. 'They're staying and so are you!' He released her arm, confident she wouldn't dare move. He towered over her, his long lean body held stiffly, ready to pounce if necessary.

Her lips felt dry and nervously she moistened them. Her head was thrown back, the chestnut curls framing the small oval of her face, the hazel eyes shimmering with sparks of green. 'I'm sick of you ordering me around!' she dared to say. 'I'm taking the children home and there's nothing you can do about it!'

'I'm warning you, Andrea,' he muttered, 'don't push me too far!'

'Don't push *you*?' she laughed bitterly. 'Oh, how cute! I'm the one who's been pushed around, slapped around, ordered about, insulted, accused and . . . and God knows what else!' she flared indignantly.

His shoulders seemed to slump and the tiredness

she had noticed before returned, giving a haggard look to the lines of his face.

'All right, Andrea, go if you must,' he sighed impatiently.

She dropped her head, confusion licking at the coils of her heart. Now that she knew she could go with the children, she found she didn't want to. 'The children have already packed their things,' she told him, as if this was of paramount importance.

He nodded. 'I'm not surprised. I'd already guessed you had this planned!'

She shifted uncomfortably, hunching a shoulder. 'Will you be all right?'

He looked at her sharply. 'What do you mean?' he growled.

'I don't know,' she shrugged, feeling miserable. 'It's just . . . well, with Hannah gone, I'm wondering if you'll be able to cope with things . . . with Sherri sick and . . . and everything,' she floundered badly, raising her hands and then dropping them helplessly at her sides. 'I'll be thinking about you,' she said then in a small voice.

'Mighty generous of you, but I could do with your help more than your thoughts!' he said, watching her closely. 'Or are you the type to desert a sinking ship?'

'Of course not! It's just—well, I thought you wanted to be alone with Sherri.' Didn't he?

His laugh was harsh. 'She's ill, for God's sake! Why would I want to be alone with her?'

Andrea chewed on her bottom lip. Her hazel eyes were dark with confusion. If Chad loved

Sherri wouldn't he want to be alone with her, especially when she was ill?

'What would you want me to do if I stayed?' she enquired.

'Well, the cooking, for one thing.'

That didn't sound so bad, she thought. 'Anything else?' she asked, to be sure.

'See to Sherri, I suppose,' he shrugged. 'Just generally making yourself useful.'

'I see,' she answered slowly, picking up the charred meat and dropping it in the rubbish. 'You want me to be Sherri's maid. When I'm not being Sherri's maid, I get to do the cooking.' She went over to the fridge and got out some fresh meat. Cutting it up, she placed it in a dish. 'When the cooking is done and Sherri has been catered to, I should look around to see what else needs doing, is that it?' she enquired sweetly as she let Bingo in for his meal.

'Something like that,' he agreed.

Andrea watched Bingo gulp down his food, before she lifted her eyes to Chad. He was leaning lazily against the fridge, ankles crossed. No man had the right to be blessed with such incredibly good looks, she fumed inwardly. Even tired as he most certainly was, he still looked crisp, fresh and rugged.

'All right,' she agreed at last. 'I'll do it, but only on one condition.'

His smile seemed to caress her whole body, starting with her face and working down. She half turned in an unconscious effort to ward off the penetration of his eyes. In two easy strides he was beside her, his huge palm lifting and holding her face. His black brows were raised inquisitively.

'What is the condition?' he asked, and to Andrea his softly spoken words were like a purr. Obviously, he too thought she was nothing but a little mouse.

Andrea swallowed hard. It was difficult trying to be tough as nails when his closeness made her feel weak and strangely vulnerable.

'The condition,' she said, 'is that we'll be even.'

A slightly sardonic smile slanted his mouth. 'What in blazes are you talking about? Even about what?'

His hand had moved from her face to rest lightly on her shoulder, but his eyes never left hers.

'The children's clothes,' she reminded him. 'Their care and the doctor's bill.' She took a deep breath. 'And the car.'

His black eyes glittered with amusement. 'Do you really think helping me out for a few days will pay for all that?'

'Yes,' she answered simply. 'Included is the price of my pride!'

Black eyes narrowed shrewdly as he studied her face. Andrea met his glance steadily, her brown eyes round and luminous.

'All right,' he agreed raggedly. 'If that's what it takes.'

Later, when Chad was upstairs with Sherri, Andrea hurried home to get a few things to tide her over for the few days she would be at the Manor. Because Chad still believed she had spent the previous night at the Manor it was left to her to choose a room. She decided on one directly across from the one the children were sharing.

The bedroom was lavishly decorated, with blue satin curtains and matching bedspread. The bed was huge, king-sized, and Andrea couldn't resist sitting on the edge, bouncing a little to try it out, but mindful not to crease the shimmering spread. She had her own connecting bathroom and fluffy yellow towels hung over a rail, their bright colour adding to the excitement of being surrounded by so much luxury. She wandered into her bedroom again, kicking off her shoes to wriggle her toes into the thick pile of the carpet. No maid ever had it so good! she thought ruefully.

Grabbing her suitcase, she swung it on to a bench and began unpacking. She hadn't brought much and she was able to carry over one arm the things which required hanging up. When she opened the wardrobe doors, she stood in astonishment, staring at the beautiful negligees hanging there. She reached out to touch one, the silky material feathery soft against her fingertips, Price tags dangled from each one and she gaped at the amounts. They certainly weren't bought at the same place she did her shopping! Pushing them aside, very carefully, of course, she made room for her slacks and blouses. She stood looking at the negligees, wondering if Chad had purchased them for his girl-friends.

Suddenly she felt very much alone. The children had been put to bed, only too eager to do as they were told in gratitude for their extended visit. Andrea hadn't seen Chad since before dinner.

When she had curtly announced that dinner was ready he had silently taken his and Sherri's up to Sherri's bedroom, leaving Andrea and the children to eat theirs in the kitchen, much to Hugo's disgust.

'Why do we have to eat in the kitchen?' he had asked, making loud noises with his soup. 'We never had to before.'

'Don't slurp your soup,' she had scolded patiently.

'But why do we?' he had insisted.

'Because we just do!'

'But why?'

'Because Chad has helped us out and now I'm helping him,' she had sighed.

'By eating in the kitchen?' he had asked, puzzled.

'No, silly, by helping with the household chores and the cooking. Things like that.'

'You're going to be Chad's maid?' Hugo asked. 'Just like Hannah?'

'Sort of,' she agreed, 'but I doubt if I'll be as efficient as Hannah.'

'Will you wear Hannah's uniform?' Melissa demanded to know.

'No,' Andrea smiled. 'At least, it hasn't been suggested . . . yet!'

'Why can't Sherri be Chad's maid?' Hugo glowered. 'Why do you have to?'

'You ask too many questions, Hugo,' Andrea answered. 'And for goodness' sakes, would you please stop slurping that soup!'

Andrea wandered aimlessly around her bedroom. It was barely nine-thirty. Surely Chad wasn't still with Sherri? she kept telling herself. She tried to fight back the jealousy that had been with her all evening. She had assumed he would eat with her and the children and had even set the table in the dining room for the occasion. But obviously he preferred Sherri's company to that of herself and Melissa and Hugo.

And why wouldn't he? she asked herself now. Sherri was so beautiful, and judging from her wardrobe and manner, obviously rich. A fatal combination, she sighed, looking at her reflection in the mirror. A dismally unhappy hazel-eyed girl stared back at her. Impulsively, Andrea reached up to flatten her hair with the palms of her hands. Sherri's hair was so smooth and sleek, and Andrea wondered how she would look as a blonde. Hideous, most likely, she sighed, releasing the chestnut curls and watching them spring back into place.

A dull ache around her heart had steadily increased all evening, and now she realised she had been living with this pain ever since Sherri had arrived on the scene. She had been a fool, she realised now, to agree to stay at the Manor. It would be nothing short of torture to be forced into watching Chad with Sherri. His devotion to the girl was obvious, and she knew she didn't have the stomach to watch him smile at her, look at her, and as Hugo and Melissa had informed her, even possibly to see him kiss her. The cruel images of Sherri in Chad's arms continued to torment her, and finally she decided a hot bath was what she needed to help erase them.

Half an hour later she emerged from the bathroom clad in one of the bright yellow towels with another wrapped turban-style around her head. She stopped short at the sight of Chad stretched out on the satin spread, his eyes watching her with devilish amusement. His black hair was damp and the black robe he was wearing told her he must have just stepped from a shower. Her eyes skimmed down his long, lean length and momentarily she panicked, thinking he had nothing on under the short bathrobe. Then with relief she caught sight of pale blue boxer shorts. Her eyes darted to the door, half expecting to see it flung open and Sherri's accusing face snarling at her. Helplessly she turned back to the imposing figure on the bed, and felt her heart fluttering in her throat. Every nerve and sense was turned upside down by his presence.

'Chad!' she whispered hoarsely. 'What . . . what are you doing here?' Her throat had constricted and it was all she could do to force the words out.

He smiled lazily and stretched. 'Resting . . . and waiting!' he drawled, his eyes wandering down her slender form, openly admiring and making her painfully aware that the towel was hardly an adequate covering.

Again her eyes darted to the closed door. 'You shouldn't be here,' she said, her voice still husky. 'Someone might come.'

He got up from the bed with the grace of a superbly fit athlete and she watched as though in a dream as he walked towards her. 'No one will come,' he drawled, the grooves on either side of his mouth deepening with amusement at Andrea's obvious discomfort. 'Everyone's in bed, asleep.'

He curved his arms around her, before she could guess that was his intention. She pressed her hands against his chest and she could feel the silky texture of black hairs.

'Chad, please!' she protested, aware of his legs against her thighs and the pleasure this contact evoked.

He smiled down at her. Her freshly scrubbed face peered up at him, tendrils of chestnut hair peeping from the confines of the yellow towel, the sweep of curling lashes framing the dark beauty of her eyes. Her lips parted at the tantalising nearness of his well-formed mouth.

Chad bent his head to brush his lips over the sweet curve of her jaw. Her nostrils quivered at the clean male scent of him and she shivered as his mouth teased the sensitive skin of her neck and shoulders.

'You know why I've come, don't you, Andrea?' he murmured, nuzzling the lobe of one pink little ear. 'You're going to be mine tonight!'

She quickly swallowed to ease the tightness in her throat, but the lump was there to stay. She moved against him, her dazed mind telling her she was resisting violently when in truth she wasn't resisting at all. It was as though his body was a live wire, sending voltages of electricity through her veins, charging every part of her until her body was fused to his in a bondage that was impossible to break.

His fingers tugged at the towel, but she didn't feel it sliding from her. His hands moved up to unwrap the turban and she was aware of his hands running through her still damp hair. Then she had the sensation of floating as he picked her up and carried her to bed. Her face had a dreamlike quality as she watched him undress, then she stretched out her arms to him as he lowered himself beside her, her body arching against his in an unbreakable hold.

When morning came, Andrea lay awake for a few minutes listening to the unfamiliar sounds of the manor coming to life. She turned sleepily on her pillow and looked at the empty pillow beside her. Was it a dream? she wondered. Had Chad really spent the night with her? She sat up in bed and looked down at her naked body. She looked the same, but she knew she would never *be* the same, ever again. Chad had made her a woman, and nothing could ever erase that and she didn't want it to.

Why did she feel so unhappy, then? she wondered as she padded barefoot across the room. Standing in front of the full-length mirror, she could see signs of their lovemaking on her body and her cheeks reddened with memory. The bathroom door opened and Chad stepped through, and smiled at her standing there. Already dressed in a pair of biege slacks and white sport shirt, he looked lean and virile. His hair was damp from his recent shower and he was a picture of masculinity.

He came up behind her, his hands moving up to gently cup her breasts, his thumbs softly stroking her nipples. 'God, but you're beautiful,' he groaned, his mouth coming down to nuzzle the curve of her shoulder.

Her breasts felt tender from his lovemaking, but even so she could feel them swelling in his hands. Desire flamed inside her, heightened by his hands which were now moving slowly down her stomach.

'Chad,' she husked, leaning against him, her eyes hooded, 'last night . . .'

'Last night was beautiful . . . you're beautiful,' he interrupted to tell her again.

He turned her around to hold her close. 'But Chad,' she said, leaning her head back to look at him, her eyes shining with the love she felt for him, 'you haven't told me you . . .'

'Desire you?' he teasingly interrupted once again. 'Well, I do, and I think I've made that fairly obvious,' he smiled, bending to kiss the tip of her nose. 'You are without doubt the most desirable, the most exciting and even the most beautiful woman I've ever known.' His smile broadened and his eyes gleamed with a devilish mockery. 'You are also the only *teacher* I've ever known!'

He didn't see the tears that hung on her lashes, frozen in place like tiny pearls. They only came after he was gone. She listened to his cheerful whistling as he made his way down the corridor then she turned to view herself in the mirror once again.

The frozen tears which hovered on her lashes finally melted. They rolled like tiny streams down her cheeks.

Desire wasn't love! Pain seared her heart. Pain so intense that she raised her hands to her chest, thinking she must surely die. It was only through supreme effort that she was able to shower and dress, forcing wooden legs down the corridor, the stairs and into the kitchen.

Chad was at the stove cooking breakfast. Any other time Andrea would have appreciated the delightful aroma of fresh bacon sizzling in the pan, of coffee percolating. But not today. Today she was only aware of how much of a fool she had been and how greatly she had been hurt.

Hugo and Melissa were helping, Hugo in charge of making toast and Melissa carefully measuring fruit juice into glasses.

'Make certain you give me just as much as you give yourself!' Hugo warned his little sister, watching closely as she poured the juice.

'Hi, kids,' Andrea greeted them in a voice she considered to be quite normal. 'Have a good rest?' she asked brightly, patting each of their heads.

'I didn't,' Hugo scowled. 'Melissa snored the whole night.'

'Did not!' Melissa denied.

'Did too,' Hugo insisted. 'Your mouth was open a mile. I felt like putting my shoe in it!'

Andrea was aware of Chad at the stove, of his deeply tanned arms shaking the pan, of the amused glances he was showering on the children. She saw all this without actually looking at him her whole attention apparently centred on Melissa and Hugo.

'Okay, you two,' he growled, 'enough of that bickering! Your sister has only just come down. Why don't one of you pour her a cup of coffee?'

The children were quick to do as they were told, obeying Chad with a willingness they hardly ever showed Andrea. She accepted the cup of coffee

Melissa handed her and sat down at the table with it, sipping slowly at the hot brew. Chad was in exceptionally good spirits, humming happily while he broke eggs into a pan. Like the cat who swallowed the mouse! Andrea thought dourly as she watched his movements from her side vision.

'My, my!' Sherri's voice drawled from the doorway. 'Isn't this a cosy scene!'

Andrea dragged her eyes over to Sherri. Dressed in white trousers and a white blazer, she resembled a snow queen with her long blonde hair streaming down her back. With barely a glance at Andrea, she strolled over to Chad and kissed him on the mouth, and Andrea felt the tight band which was constricting her heart tighten even further.

'Darling!' Sherri pouted, her blue eyes rounded in childish innocence as she gazed up at Chad. 'Must *you* perform these mundane chores? I thought you hired Andy to do them?'

Sherri's blue eyes slid over to Andrea sitting at the table. Andrea avoided her glance by rolling up the sleeves of her rust-coloured jumper, knowing Sherri had deliberately used her nickname as an intended slight.

'I didn't *hire* Andy,' Chad corrected her, amused.

'No-o-o?' Sherri drawled, taking her place at the table across from Andrea, and Andrea could feel her gaze slicing into her, dissecting her into a million little pieces. 'If you didn't hire her, why is she here?'

They were discussing her as though she wasn't even in the kitchen! Andrea felt the blood rush to her cheeks and at that moment she couldn't decide who she hated more, Sherri or Chad, and then generously decided she hated them both equally. She waited for Chad's answer.

But Sherri wasn't particularly interested in answers. She still had questions of her own. 'Chad,' she said, looking up at him while he placed platters of egg and bacon on the table, 'where did you sleep last night?'

Andrea felt herself stiffening and her throat went dry. Her back was rigid as she darted stricken looks at the children who were listening curiously and to Chad who didn't seem disturbed in the least by Sherri's all too obvious question.

'Well, I certainly didn't sleep in the garage,' he laughed.

'Nor in your bed!' Sherri snapped. 'I heard something during the night and I went to your room. You weren't there!'

Andrea felt herself shivering at the frosty look he passed to Sherri, grateful that it wasn't directed at her. At least not this time.

'I heard something, too,' he told her coldly. 'You must have come to my room when I was investigating.'

'I know what you musta heard,' Hugo told Sherri. 'It musta been Melissa snoring!'

Sherri looked at Hugo with obvious distaste. 'Oh, shut up!' she snapped.

CHAPTER TEN

THE next morning after breakfast Chad took Sherri and the children for a drive. Hugo and Melissa returned happy after the excursion, but Sherri looked cross and annoyed. Andrea had been invited to join the group but had refused, claiming there was much to be done at the Manor, and she was determined that when she left her debt would be paid in full.

The group had crowded in the kitchen where Andrea was polishing some silver at the table.

'Do you mind if we make some hot chocolate?' asked Chad, smiling at her while she scrubbed furiously at the silver.

'Of course not,' she answered, feeling her cheeks grow hot. 'Why should I? It's your chocolate and your kitchen,' she added, feeling Sherri's hateful glare on her.

'Let Andrea make the chocolate, Chad,' Sherri suggested, entwining her arm in his. 'She can serve it to us in the sun room.' She smiled appealingly up at Chad. 'It's so beautiful in there this time of day.'

Andrea got up from the table to wash her hands at the sink. 'Good idea,' she said. 'Why don't all of you go in there now and I'll bring it in as soon as it's ready.'

Chad disentangled himself from Sherri's grasp and strode over to Andrea at the sink. 'Don't be

172

ridiculous,' he snapped, but she refused to acknowl-
edge the warning note in his voice. 'I think you're
carrying this "maid" bit a little too far. I wouldn't
expect Hannah to drop everything just to make a
drink, and I certainly don't expect you to.'

Andrea whirled from the sink to face him, her
hazel eyes unnaturally bright. 'Really?' she asked.
'Well, that's good, because I'd like to get the dining
room furniture dusted before I put the silver back.
I've done the vacuuming upstairs, but I haven't
had a chance to do downstairs, so if you could
make your own hot chocolate it would really
help!'

With that, she dried her hands and marched
stiffly from the kitchen.

'Don't worry about Andy,' she heard Hugo say.
'She always gets in a pickle when she knows she's
got vacuuming to do.'

'I wouldn't put up with it, Chad . . .' came
Sherri's voice, but Andrea didn't hang around long
enough to hear the remainder of her sentence.
She'd find a way to get even with Hugo for his little
remark, she thought, though. The monster!

As she vacuumed the dining room she was grateful she only had one more day left to repay her debt
and then she would be free. She didn't think her
nerves could tolerate much more of constantly
avoiding Chad. She knew he was puzzled by her
behaviour and often she had felt those black eyes
on her. In a way she was even grateful for Sherri's
presence at the Manor, for when Chad wasn't
working in his den, Sherri was constantly by his
side.

Meal times were perhaps the worst, because then she was forced into direct contact with Chad, and often it seemed no matter where she looked, her eyes would invariably fall on his. But once again Sherri unwittingly came to the rescue. Conversation was impossible owing to her constant chattering about her friends, her and Chad's mutual friends, stories about their divorces or impending separations, who was having an affair with whom and for what reasons and did you really blame them, and so on and so on.

When Sherri wasn't predicting gloom and doom, then Hugo and Melissa filled in the gaps with bits and pieces of their own. Throughout all this Chad watched Andrea, his eyes mocking her with sardonic amusement, so that the mere act of swallowing food became almost an impossibility.

Andrea had almost finished in the dining room when Sherri came into the room, her cheeks red and her eyes blazing with anger.

'I thought you said you'd done the upstairs!' she accused Andrea.

'I have,' answered Andrea as she lifted the silver tea service from the table to place on the buffet.

'Well, you haven't done my room,' Sherri lashed out. 'My bed hasn't been made, and you didn't make it yesterday either!'

Andrea stared at her. 'Surely you don't expect me to make your bed?' she gasped.

'Of course I do. I complained to Chad about it yesterday, but I didn't think it would be necessary to do it again today.'

'Well, I'm afraid that's exactly what you will have

to do, because I have no intention of making your bed today, just as I didn't yesterday!'

Sherri's eyes narrowed into slits. 'I left a bundle of clothing in my room to be washed. I see you haven't done *that* either.'

'No, I don't go around searching for things to be washed,' Andrea told her patiently, 'but if you care to leave them in the laundry room, I'll put them in with the next load.'

Sherri's eyes flew open in disbelief. 'The next *load*!' she squealed. 'You mean the *washing machine*?'

'Of course.' Andrea bent down to pick up the vacuum cleaner. 'I've already done a wash today, but the children will most likely have stuff that needs doing tomorrow, so if yours is there I'll drop it in.'

Sherri sank into one of the dining room chairs, staring up at Andrea as though she had suddenly developed two heads. 'My finery . . . in a washing machine? With their *filthy* clothes?'

Andrea shrugged. 'You can always do it yourself,' she suggested, walking towards the door.

Sherri recovered sufficiently to jump up from her chair and run after her, blocking off the door. 'Don't think you're going to get away with this,' she hissed, 'because you won't—I'll see to that!'

'Just see to your wash, Sherri,' Andrea replied patiently. 'Now, if you'll get out of my way, I've still got some more work to do.'

Sherri leaned against the door, a cruel smile playing along her lips. 'You're doing such a fine job here,' she said, 'that I wouldn't be surprised if Chad suggested you stay on to help Hannah while we're on our honeymoon.' She waited while her words took effect, watching the wounded look in Andrea's eyes with malicious glee. 'Oh, didn't you know?' she continued, with a smile. 'It won't be long now before Chad and I are married.' She walked away from the door, confident that Andrea would stay. 'You would like that, wouldn't you, Andrea? Dusting and cleaning Chad's possessions while he and I are off on our honeymoon?' She picked up a silver sugar bowl, examined it and then placed it back on the tray. 'After all, even with Chad and myself away, the Manor is a big place to take care of . . . far too big for Hannah, and her niece isn't that much help.' She whirled to face Andrea. 'But you are, aren't you?' she sneered. 'So eager and willing to please . . . in and out of bed!'

'You don't know what you're talking about, Sherri,' Andrea sighed. 'I'm helping Chad because he helped me—it's as simple as that.'

Sherri laughed, a cruel hard sound. 'And you must think I'm simple if you expect me to believe you! Anyway,' she went on, running her fingers over the smooth top of the dining table, 'aren't you going to congratulate me on my engagement, or do you think you still have a chance with Chad?'

'I was never in the running for him,' Andrea shrugged, her eyes on Sherri's left hand.

Sherri held up her hand. 'You're wondering where my ring is, aren't you? Well, I haven't been able to decide on one yet. Chad thinks rubies and emeralds, but I think perhaps diamonds. After all, diamonds are forever!' she gloated.

'You might try a compromise,' Andrea suggested weakly. 'It's not uncommon nowadays to see an engagement ring with all three stones.' What was she doing, she wondered, discussing Sherri's engagement to the man she loved? What had she ever done to deserve such cruel punishment? But Sherri wasn't through with her yet.

'Yes,' she agreed, holding up her hand and looking at her finger as though the ring was already there, 'that would be nice, and Chad could certainly afford it.' She dropped her hand as though suddenly bored with the whole idea. 'By the way, *Andy*, don't think you'll be working here *after* our honeymoon—I wouldn't want Chad sneaking from my bed to yours!' She laughed at the stricken look that crossed Andrea's face. 'I've forgiven him for the other night,' she cooed. 'I realise men do those sorts of things just before they get married. I think it's called sowing their wild oats . . . something like that!'

Andrea somehow managed to get through that day, although she was never able to remember afterwards just how she had spent her time. She had accepted the fact that Chad didn't love her, long before Sherri spelt it out to her. What hurt her the most was the realisation that Chad had used her to betray Sherri. He had made love to her while his betrothed lay in another bedroom just down the landing. She felt soiled, used—and even worse, bitterly disappointed that Chad, the man she loved, had broken a promise to the girl he was engaged to.

That evening she worked on school reports in the

downstairs reading room. She worked until almost midnight, exhausting herself to keep herself from thinking about Chad and Sherri and her own horrible part in their relationship, She wanted to be so tired that when her head hit the pillow, she would go straight to sleep. Her only comfort was in knowing the next day was Tuesday and she would be free to leave. Her debt would be paid and then she would take the children and move from the valley. With luck she would never see Chad or Sherri again—and she knew for certain she would never read another one of Chad's books!

With the last of the reports done, she tucked them into her briefcase, then went into the kitchen for a glass of milk and to give Bingo his nightly biscuit. She was on her knees patting the dog when Chad came into the kitchen. Thinking she was the only one still up, she had no reason not to let the tears that had threatened to betray her the whole day fall on Bingo's silky head.

Her expression was unguarded when she looked up to find Chad standing in the doorway, watching her. Quickly she rose to her feet, swiping at her cheeks with the palms of her hands.

'I . . . I didn't think anyone was still up,' she faltered, saying the first words that came into her mind.

'Nor did I,' he smiled, watching her. 'I came down for a glass of milk. I saw the light on in the kitchen.'

'I was doing some school work in the reading room,' she explained. 'I came in for a glass of milk, too.'

'And to give Bingo his biscuit?' he enquired.

'Yes, and to . . . to pat him.'

She waited for him to say something about the fact that she had been crying, but he didn't, and she began to breathe easier. 'I'll pour you a glass of milk,' she volunteered, reaching for the jug still on the counter beside her. 'There's some cake left over from dinner,' she said, passing him the glass of milk. 'Would you like some of that?'

'No, thanks. The milk will do nicely,' said Chad, taking the glass with one hand and rubbing the muscles of his neck with the other. 'It's almost midnight,' he told her. 'You should be in bed.' His gaze scanned her face, settling on her eyes and the dark smudges underneath. 'You've been working too hard, Andrea. I would never have agreed to this ridiculous idea of yours to repay what you thought you owed me, had I known what it was going to cost you.'

She turned away from him, unable to meet his eyes. He would never know what it had cost her to remain at the Manor knowing he and Sherri were engaged to be married. He swung her around to face him. 'I had a telephone call from Hannah this afternoon,' he said. 'Apparently there are so many relatives on hand to look after her sister-in-law that she feels she would be more useful here. When I told her you'd taken charge, doing all the work, she exploded over the phone. I wouldn't be surprised if she boxed my ears tomorrow when I pick her up!' He smiled down at her, his fingers lightly tracing the collar of her white shirt, his hands moving up her neck to run through the sweep of chestnut curls.

'Don't!' she gasped, rearing her head away from him. 'D-don't touch me like that!'

His hands moved from her head to settle on her shoulders and she could feel the heat from them burning through to her flesh. The smile on his face was sad, troubled.

'What's wrong, Andrea?' he asked softly, his eyes searching her face. 'You must know how I feel about you, yet . . . yet you act so cold, distant.' He frowned. 'You haven't smiled since you've been here and you've avoided me at every turn. Is it Sherri?' he asked now. 'Has she done something to upset you?'

Andrea shrugged out of his grip, two bright spots of red burning like hot coals in her cheeks. How typically arrogant for him to assume the fault lay with someone else! Yes, Sherri had upset her all right, but not nearly as much as he had.

'You said—' she swallowed hard, 'you said my debt would be repaid if I helped out for a few days?'

He stuffed his hands into his pockets and nodded. 'Yes, that's what we agreed upon,' he answered quietly.

'Tomorrow is Tuesday . . . my last day.'

He nodded again. 'Yes, and Hannah comes back tomorrow, or should I say today?' he smiled, looking at the kitchen clock. 'It's well past midnight.'

Andrea turned to pick up the jug of milk and to carry it over to the fridge. Chad opened the door for her and she slid it into its place, the cool blast of air fanning her fevered cheeks before he closed it again. She quickly retraced her steps back over to the counter, desperately in need to keep a safe distance between them.

'I'll be leaving tomorrow, then,' she said in a small voice, breathless with the heady sensation of just being near him. Her treacherous body had betrayed her before and her brain told her she was heading for certain disaster if she allowed herself to remain anywhere near him.

The black eyes searched her face, but she looked quickly away, terrified he might read the truth of her thoughts.

'There's no need for you to go home tomorrow,' he said. 'Why not make it easy on yourself and stay at least until the end of the week? With Hannah here, there won't be anything for you to do, and you did say this was a busy time for you at school.'

She shook her head. 'No, you don't understand,' she said quietly. 'I'm leaving the valley . . . not just the Manor. I . . . I've made all the arrangements,' she hurried on, feeling the need to get this over quickly. 'I have friends in Hobart who can put the children and myself up for a few days, or at least until I can find suitable accommodation for us.'

She wasn't prepared for his reaction, for the cold, angry look that gleamed from his eyes, from lips that became tightly compressed. Wary of his flashpoint anger, she took a step backwards, certain he might strike her, or worse. He strode towards her, grasping her wrist.

'*Why?*' he rasped, his grip tightening to the point of agony, and she knew then that she had prodded a sleeping devil. He drew her closer to him, his eyes searing her face. '*Why*, for God's sake, can you tell me *why*? You love the valley.'

Helplessly she gazed up at him, feeling the thudding of his heart against her own. 'It's for the best,' she managed to gasp, wincing as he tightened his grip even more. 'The children are getting bigger . . . they need more. If we l-live in Hobart, I can get a full-time teaching job. It's for the best,' she repeated, as if this told him everything.

Chad dropped her hand and she rubbed it, watching him. There would be a bruise by morning, she knew, but at least *this* bruise would be easily seen. Her heart would be bruised for ever without anyone ever knowing!

His eyes roamed over her and she stood perfectly still. He seemed to examine her in great detail, starting from the top of her head to the tips of her toes. Finally he shrugged. 'You're probably right!' he agreed, and she watched as he turned and walked from the kitchen as though she no longer existed.

Andrea dragged herself around the Manor the whole of the following day getting everything in order for Hannah's return. Fortunately Chad and Sherri weren't there, and where they had gone Andrea didn't particularly care. She was only grateful she didn't have to suffer through any more of Sherri's nasty remarks, or have her heart torn out every time she saw Chad.

Hugo and Melissa were far from happy when she told them they would be moving to Hobart. Patiently, she told them how a full-time job meant more money and she needed this extra money if she was to care for them properly. But they remained unimpressed, insisting that Chad would take care of them whenever they needed it.

'Chad will have Sherri to care for,' she explained. 'I don't think he'll need any extra responsibility.'

'Is Chad going to *marry* Sherri?' Hugo asked incredulously.

'It rather looks that way,' Andrea answered, forcing a brightness into her voice for the children's benefit.

'But we thought he was going to marry *us*!' Melissa sniffed, starting to cry. 'Hugo said everything was going according to plan.'

Andrea whirled towards Hugo. '*What?*'

Hugo shifted uncomfortably, avoiding her eyes. 'I planned for Chad to marry you, and he probably woulda if you'd had blonde hair!'

'Like Sherri's,' Melissa sniffed. 'I told Hugo gentlemen prefer blondes, but he wouldn't listen. He said you had a few blonde pieces of hair on your head and that it would be enough, but it wasn't,' she continued sadly.

Andrea knelt in front of them, taking each little hand in her own. 'Listen, you two,' she scolded gently. 'Chad wouldn't marry Sherri just because she has blonde hair. He's marrying her because he . . . because he—well, because he loves her,' she finally managed to get the dreaded words out.

'Well, can we at least stay here until Chad gets back?' Hugo pleaded. 'Maybe I can talk him out of Sherri and into marrying you!' he added hopefully. 'I don't think I would want to visit Chad too often if

Sherri was his wife,' he sighed wistfully. 'She doesn't seem to like us all that much.'

Andrea smiled and ruffled his hair. 'If they're back before five then you can say goodbye, but you must promise not to mention anything to Chad about this little conversation!' she warned.

But Chad wasn't back by five, nor was he back by six. Finally at seven o'clock Andrea announced to the children that they must leave. 'It's already too late to drive into Hobart tonight,' she said, 'and I don't want us staying another night here. You're both tired. We'd better go home.'

'But what about Hannah?' asked Melissa. 'Hannah will be sad to find us gone.'

'I know, darling, but they must have got held up. You and Hugo can write a "thank you" note to Hannah after we get settled in our new place.'

'But can't we come back here in the morning?' Hugo pleaded. 'I like to say my "thank you's" face to face!'

'I'm afraid not,' Andrea sighed wearily. 'We'll be gone by first light.'

With a last check to make certain everything was perfect, she finally managed to get the children bundled into her little car. As they waved a tearful farewell to the empty Manor, Andrea couldn't help but wonder how one man could have altered their lives so completely.

Their own little house was freezing cold and damp after having been locked up for so many days. Andrea quickly got the slow-combustion stove going and lit a fire in the lounge, while the children got ready for bed. The fireplace in the lounge smoked a little, but then managed to clear itself up, drawing better than Andrea could ever remember it doing before.

With the children asleep she decided she had better let her friends in Hobart know she wouldn't be coming tonight so they wouldn't be worrying about her. It was a clear night, so she decided to walk to the phone booth, leaving her car parked in the driveway where it was.

As she walked along the deserted street, she bade a silent farewell to the little village, and tomorrow she would do the same to the valley. She supposed that in time her wounds would heal and she would one day be able to come back here, but she didn't think that time would come in the very near future. With her phone call made, she stepped out of the phone booth, breathing in the fresh sweet air in great choking sobs. Then, straightening her shoulders with fresh determination, she made her way back to the little house.

From the bottom of their lane, she could see their house. She had left the lights on downstairs, but she couldn't remember leaving any on upstairs. Either Hugo or Melissa must have got up to use the bathroom and left the light burning, she decided, but as she got closer she became puzzled by the colour of the light. The lights downstairs appeared bright yellow, but the light burning upstairs was a dirty orange.

As she watched, the light seemed to flicker, disappear for a second or two and then reappear a much brighter orange. She began walking faster, then broke into a run, her eyes wide with horror as she finally realised what it was. *The house was on fire!*

Run, Andy, run! a voice inside her chanted. *Run, Andy, run!* But she couldn't seem to run fast enough. Her legs felt like dead weights as she dragged them after her. *Run, Andy, run!* the voice continued to chant. Run *faster*, Andy! *Faster!* Faster, Andy, or you'll be too late! *Too late to save the children!*

Her breath came in ragged gasps as the voice inside her urged her on and her eyes never left the horror of the orange flames dancing behind the windowpanes. The lazy flames licked out and caught the curtains, turning them into raging torches. As she got closer she could hear the glass popping from their frames and splintering glass was sprayed in all directions as the windows exploded under the intense heat.

She tore towards the direction of the door, not feeling the heat, not seeing the flames, knowing only that Hugo and Melissa were trapped inside, and she imagined she heard them screaming for her to save them. Then she felt small hands clutching at her and looked down to see them, their beautiful little faces blackened by soot.

'You're safe!' she sobbed uncontrollably. 'You're safe!' She clutched them to her, her hands running over their bodies as if to convince herself they were truly there.

'Chad saved us!' Hugo screamed above the roar of the fire. 'He's gone back in there looking for you. He thinks you're in the house!'

Time seemed suspended as Hugo's words sank in

and Andrea felt all life draining from her body. Chad! In slow motion her head turned towards the house. Flames were pouring from all the windows now and even from where they stood the heat was unbearable. Chad!

'Get back!' she screamed to the children, pushing them towards the road. 'Get back!' Then she turned and raced towards the burning house. Chad! Somewhere inside was the man she loved, facing almost certain death in his search to find her. Chad! Flames were licking at the door as she kicked it open. Somewhere in the distance she could hear a fire siren, but they would be too late!

'Chad!' she screamed, and smoke filled her lungs, making her feel nauseated and dizzy. She doubled over, inching her way towards the lounge, memory her only guide as she stumbled through the thick black smoke. 'Chad!' she screamed over and over again. 'My darling, my love! Where are you?'

The ceiling above her collapsed, rafters and embers spraying in all directions. It was then she saw him, his clothes alight and his eyes two burning orbs in his face. She saw his hand reach out for her, heard her name come from his lips, and then their world exploded around them, drowning out all sight, all sound except an earth shattering scream as once more she called his name. 'C-h-a-a-a-d-d-d!'

It was a miracle, everyone said, that no one had lost their lives in that fire. Chad had reached Andrea just in the nick of time, carrying her to safety only seconds before the house crumbled into a fiery heap. No one was even hurt, another miracle, so everyone said—and so it was. But the biggest miracle of all was how, from the fiery depths of hell Chad and Andrea emerged into their own special heaven.

In Chad's upstairs den, Andrea and he stood by the window looking across the meadow to where the little house had once stood. Incredibly, smoke could still be seen rising from the embers. 'This is where I used to stand,' Chad told her softly, 'and look across to the house, wondering and worrying what you were doing.' He smiled down at her, his arm around her shoulders tightening into a more protective grip. 'Last night when I got home I came up here to look across. That's when I saw the flames. I can't remember how I got there, all I knew was that I had to get to you fast.'

She rested her head against his shoulder, snuggling into its warmth. 'We waited for you until after seven,' she murmured softly. 'The children wanted to say goodbye.'

'But not you?' he asked, his voice gently teasing.

She shook her head. 'I don't think I could have stood it,' she answered honestly. 'Oh, Chad, why didn't you explain to me about Sherri before?' she condemned. 'If you only knew how it broke my heart, thinking you were about to marry her!'

He kissed the tip of her nose, her eyelids and then her mouth before answering. 'I realised she was up to mischief, but it wasn't until I got her to the airport for her flight back home to Sydney that she finally revealed what she'd told you. I could have wrung her neck, and if her parents weren't such good friends of mine and if I hadn't promised to take care of her, that's probably exactly what I would have done!'

He picked her up and carried her over to the sofa. 'Let's not waste any more time discussing Sherri,' he told her gruffly. 'We've wasted enough time already, and if I live to be a hundred it won't be long enough to show you how much I love you.'

I love you! Three little words, three precious little words. 'Oh, Chad,' whispered Andrea, 'how I've longed to hear you say that!'

He took her face in his hands and smiled at her tenderly. 'I've loved you from the beginning,' he told her. 'Since we accidentally met in the street. It just took me a long time to realise it, that's all. Perhaps Sherri, in her own way, even helped to spur things on a bit. If it hadn't been for her, you might not have decided to leave the valley. It was the idea of you leaving that made me realise life without you would be unbearable.'

'If I had made it to Hobart,' she teased, 'how would you have found me? After all, I've never told you which school I teach at.'

'I would have torn the city apart looking for you. I would have visited every school, I would have haunted the streets, I wouldn't have stopped till I found you.' He smiled down at her, his eyes filled with the love he felt for her. 'But none of that would have been necessary,' he said then, 'because I'd planned to stop you in the morning before you even drove out your driveway.'

She sat up straight. 'But how did you know we were leaving in the morning?' she asked. 'I never told you . . . did I? I just said we were leaving, I didn't say when.'

'Hugo left me a note,' he explained, laughter lighting his eyes. 'He told me to make sure I got there at first light.'

'Why, that little imp!' she laughed, snuggling her face into his neck. After a while, as he rocked her gently in his arms, she asked him, 'Where are the children now? I've hardly seen them all day.'

'They're cleaning up a little surprise for you. I told them to come up when they'd finished with it.'

'A surprise? For me?'

Just then the door flew open and Hugo, followed by Melissa, came into the den. 'Close your eyes and hold out your hands,' he commanded, and when Andrea had done as she was bid, he placed the surprise in her hands. 'Now open your eyes,' the children chorussed together.

Andrea opened her eyes to see the family portrait lying in her hands. It had a new frame and new glass, but the picture itself had not been damaged. She raised her eyes to the children and then to Chad. Tears swam in her eyes. 'Oh, thank you,' she whispered to all of them. 'I . . . I thought this had been lost in the fire.'

'Chad saved it for us,' Hugo told her stoutly. 'He had it hidden under his jumper when he carried you out of the house. So it looks like he saved all of us, eh, Andy? The whole family.'

Andrea reached across to lay her hand across the fair curls. 'It sure looks that way,' she agreed with a smile.

The children took the portrait down to show